L5792m

The Magic Hat of Mortimer Wintergreen

MYRON LEVOY
The Magic Hat of Mortimer Wintergreen

A CHARLOTTE ZOLOTOW BOOK
CZ

Harper & Row, Publishers

Library of Congress Cataloging-in-Publication Data
Levoy, Myron.
    The magic hat of Mortimer Wintergreen.

    "A Charlotte Zolotow book."
    Summary: In 1893, thirteen-year-old Joshua and his
eleven-year-old sister, Amy, travel from South Dakota
to New York City with the help of the mysterious Mor-
timer Wintergreen and his unpredictable magic hat.
    [1. Magicians—Fiction.   2. Voyages and travels—
Fiction.   3. Orphans—Fiction.   4. Humorous stories]
I. Title.
PZ7.L5825Mag   1988   [Fic]   87-45292
ISBN 0-06-023841-0
ISBN 0-06-023842-9 (lib. bdg.)

For Bea

CONTENTS

The Magic Hat of Mortimer Wintergreen

1. THE TRAGIC MAGIC SHOW

Amy and Joshua Baines slipped through a side window, stepped lightly over the creaky porch boards, then ran down the road toward town. They had seen the posters yesterday:

THE INCREDIBLE WINTERGREEN.

THE GREATEST MAGICIAN

IN THE ENTIRE AMERICAN CONTINENT.

COME ONE, COME ALL.

JULY 28TH, 1893. FOUR P.M. IN BENSON'S BARN.

ADMISSION: EIGHTEEN CENTS ADULTS;

NINE CENTS CHILDREN UNDER FOURTEEN.

CATS AND DOGS ONE CENT

IF ON LEASH OR HELD FIRMLY.

They knew Aunt Vootch would punish them when they returned. She always did.

Her punishments came as regularly as sunup and sundown, her anger bursting like dark storms over the cornfields. But for the moment they were free, and Aunt Vootch would have to rage alone.

As they ran, Amy saw Benson's barn in the distance, beyond a field of tall grass. "Race you to the barn, Josh!" she shouted. "Bet you a penny I beat you!"

"A nickel!" shouted Joshua. "A nickel says you couldn't beat a three-legged coughing cow!"

"Okay! It's a bet!"

Joshua was thirteen and Amy was eleven, but they were equally matched in running because Joshua was short for his age and Amy was tall. Still, Joshua usually managed to win, mainly by shouting at Amy that she was going to lose, was losing, had lost.

They sped across Benson's field, straight toward the crowd gathered at the shady side of the barn. "You're losing!" shouted Joshua. "Look at you, losing! Amy Baines is losing!" Then he stumbled in an old wagon rut, while Amy dashed into the crowd.

"You owe me a nickel!" she called.

The crowd parted to make way for them, as if they were famous outlaws who had just escaped from jail.

"Poor things," said Mrs. Benson. "They must have gone through the window again."

"I hear that aunt of theirs is the meanest woman in South Dakota," a man in tattered blue overalls said.

I'm *not* a poor thing, thought Joshua. He couldn't explain why, but he found himself defending his aunt. "Aw, she's just crazy in her head 'cause her stepfather used to beat her. That's what my ma told me a long time ago."

"You generous, generous forgiving child," said Mrs. Benson, as she kissed Joshua on the forehead.

Things could be worse, thought Joshua. At least Aunt Vootch didn't go around kissing people. Ever.

Amy frowned. "I don't forgive her at all," she said. She stared at Joshua defiantly, but Joshua just shrugged.

At that moment, they heard someone near

the barn calling, "Tickets, ladies and gentle-men! Purchase your tickets here! Do not stampede, if you please. Form a neat line."

They turned and saw a rather stout man with a thin gray mustache standing on a sag-ging bale of hay. He wore an elegant blue jacket with a checkered vest beneath, and a pair of spotless white gloves. The man was busily handing out tickets. With every sale, he tipped his hat and said, "We thank you kindly."

As the crowd surged ahead into the barn, Amy and Joshua moved forward until they were in front of the ticket seller. "Aha," the man said to Joshua. "You look about seven and the lady must be about fourteen and a half. Making one adult and one child."

"But I'm only eleven," Amy said.

"And I'm thirteen!" said Joshua indig-nantly. Everyone always thought he was younger. The boys at school made fun of him and bullied him because he was so short. It wasn't fair! Why did Amy have to get all the height?

"You're thirteen?" the man asked. "Why

haven't you been drinking my tonic, young man? Wintergreen's All-Season Health Tonic, for the growing youth." He took a little brown bottle and thrust it into Joshua's palm. "There you are. That'll be thirty-five cents."

"I don't have thirty-five cents," said Joshua.

"Ah . . . Well, well . . . But wait! Yours is the hundredth ticket. Congratulations! You get this bottle for free. Now on to business. Two children-sized admissions. Nine cents and nine cents. Here are your tickets, and please hold any dogs and cats firmly. They spoil my tricks."

"Are you Mr. Wintergreen?" asked Amy. "Josh, look! He's the magician! He's a real magician!"

"Okay, I see," said Joshua, still unhappy at being mistaken for a seven-year-old.

Wintergreen tipped his hat. "Pleasure's all mine. Thank you for your kindly patronage. Next please. Step right up. The show goes on in two minutes."

Joshua and Amy hurried into the cool, dark barn. There were chairs at one end and a small raised platform in front. The seats were almost full, but they managed to find two places in the third row.

A few more people scurried to find seats. Then Mortimer Wintergreen stepped onto the platform and bowed. "Ladies and gentlemen, children, cats, and dogs. I would like your careful attention. You are about to see the most incredible trick in the history of North America. Observe. There is absolutely nothing up my sleeves. Now then. Watch!"

Mortimer took off his gray silk top hat, held it out so everyone could see inside, then tapped it three times with his wand. He began pulling colored silk handkerchiefs from the hat, one after another: red, blue, yellow, orange.

A man in the audience shouted, "Hey! I saw a magician do that back in Rapid City! It's easy! The hat's got a secret compartment. Show us a new one!"

"Ah," said Mortimer. "Doubts being raised. Well, well. Let's see what else we have."

He reached deep into the hat, then slowly pulled out a length of frayed rope. At first there was scattered laughter from the audience. But more rope emerged, and still more. The audience watched intently.

Amy looked at Joshua in amazement. "I'm glad we came," she whispered. "This is the best trick I've ever seen."

"Look!" Joshua whispered. "The rope's still coming out! How does he do it?"

"My, my. Can't seem to get to the end of this rope," said the magician, as it fell in large coils at his feet. The audience was absolutely silent now. And when the other end of the rope finally popped out, with a wet towel hanging from it, they applauded wildly.

"Thank you, my friends," said Wintergreen. "Is the gentleman from Rapid City satisfied? That trick alone was worth the price of admission. Now on to something new—"

Just then, a woman carrying a wet tablecloth rushed into the barn. "My clothesline!" she shouted. "He stole my clothesline from under my nose! I saw it going across the field! I saw it being pulled all the way here!"

"Ah me. Ah me," murmured Wintergreen. "That hat! It's done it again."

The woman pointed to the rope on the platform. "He's wrecked my clothesline!"

"Now, now, madam," said the magician. "I will positively pay you for your clothesline at the end of this performance."

"Well," said the woman. "If you'll pay . . ."

"Yes, indeed. And you'll receive a free bottle of my famous Wintergreen's All-Season Health Tonic, as well. Thank you kindly. And now, let's try another little trick. Ladies and gentlemen, cats, dogs, *and* clothesline owners, I am going to carry this hat into the audience. You will observe that there is absolutely nothing in it, on it, or around it. . . ."

Wintergreen walked through the audience, showing his hat to left and right. Joshua stood on his seat to see; the hat was completely empty.

"I am now going to dip my hand into this hat and remove something," said Wintergreen, as he returned to the platform. "I will not tell you what. It will be a complete surprise. It might be a jeweled crown. It may be a statue of George Washington. It could be a box of nails. Or a feather duster. Get ready! Prepare! Here—it—comes!"

Amy and Joshua and the entire audience leaned forward. Slowly Wintergreen's hand went down into the hat. Slowly it came back up. And in his hand was a live skunk!

"Oh no! Not again. Ah me," said Wintergreen sadly. "Well, well, folks. Look what we have. A furry friend."

At that moment the skunk, frightened by the audience, defended itself by releasing its oily odor. Within a few seconds, the barn smelled right through the roof to the blue sky above. The crowd rushed to the door as if they were one person, and leading them all was none other than Mortimer Wintergreen, magician.

Unfortunately, Aunt Vootch had just arrived at the barn door carrying her buggy whip. "So!" she shouted. "Where are those children?" Then she saw Wintergreen at the head of the crowd. "Steal my help in the middle of the day, will you!"

Down came her whip on Wintergreen's back as he ran toward his horse and wagon. And as he raced away, Aunt Vootch began whipping everyone who tried to come through the door.

"Idlers! Loafers! You should all be working!"

The crowd finally escaped from Aunt Vootch and the skunk through the other end of the barn. But Amy and Joshua stayed behind, though the smell of skunk brought tears to their eyes and made them choke and gag. They hid in the hayloft and were glad to be there, for Aunt Vootch's punishments were worse than the smell of any skunk in South Dakota.

2. THE PIGPEN SPECIAL

my and Joshua had lived with Aunt Vootch ever since their parents had been accidently shot by cavalrymen far out on the prairie, near Larison's Creek. Their father and mother had been searching for a stray pony and, in the evening shadows, had been mistaken for Indians. It was the year of the Ghost Dance, the year the Sioux had risen in one last desperate attempt to regain their past way of life, and every cavalryman in South Dakota had one hand on his gun, even when he was asleep. Afterward the captain of the cavalry had sent Joshua and Amy a pair of silver-plated six-shooters with engraving on the barrels which read: *For Amy and Josh, real straight shooters, both. In sad memory of their dearly beloved parents. The Battle of Larison's Creek, November 21, 1890.*

From the very first day Joshua and Amy came to live with her, Aunt Vootch nailed lists of chores to the kitchen wall. She would lie on the settee having a headache, while she held up large cards with numbers on them. Every number matched a job on the list. Three meant feed the chickens. Eighteen meant scrub the kitchen floor. Twenty meant fetch water.

And thirteen meant punishment time. Sometimes she would force them to write "I will do as I am told" over and over on a slate, till the chalk wore down to their fingernails. Sometimes she'd make them dig post holes in the hot summer sun. And sometimes she would just shout at them—her face turning red, then blue—until she fell back on the settee, exhausted from her angry fit.

Now, as she searched in Benson's barn, she prodded and probed the mounds of hay with her whip, a great black one with a delicate rose design on the handle. Above her, in the loft, Amy and Joshua didn't dare make the slightest sound. They couldn't even say *phew* to the skunk smell as they dug down deeper into the hay.

A minute or two passed, and then Aunt Vootch called out, "Amy, Joshuaaaa! Where are you? Children must have an afternoon off from time to time. Auntie Vootch understands. No punishment."

"She's lying," Amy whispered to Joshua. "Sticky lying, like flypaper."

"*Sssh!*" Joshua moved forward slightly. "Let me listen. I can tell if she means it from how she sounds."

"Children! I know you're in here. So take a peek. I have something for you. Surprise!"

"I'm going to look," Joshua whispered. He slid slowly to the edge of the loft, keeping under the hay. Then he looked down and saw Aunt Vootch, below, holding up a seven card in each hand. He crawled back to Amy and whispered, "Double sevens. It means we get chocolate cake *and* lemonade for supper."

"Do you believe it?" asked Amy.

"Yes. She's never gone back on her numbers. Let's surrender before the skunk smell kills us dead." And they both jumped up, sending a shower of hay to the ground below.

"There you are!" called Aunt Vootch. "Now come home for supper, children. The cake and lemonade are all ready."

Aunt Vootch didn't say another word to them, but she did hum a little tune as if she were quite pleased with herself as they climbed into her buggy. This was another treat; they rarely had a chance to ride in her buggy. Even when they tried to just sit in it for a moment, the big black horse, Orion, would buck and kick.

Aunt Vootch hummed all the way home and all through supper. She let Amy and Joshua have all the chocolate cake they could eat and two pitchers of lemonade with cherry syrup.

"Eat up, children. Don't leave any," she said. Then she sang to herself, "La la tee da la, tum tum tee la la . . ."

After Amy had had her third helping of chocolate cake, she whispered to Joshua, "Josh, I think she's gone totally crazy. Orion must have kicked her right in the head."

"Eat up, eat up," sang Aunt Vootch. "Eat up, up, up te da la, te dum dum . . ."

At last Amy and Joshua had eaten as much

cake as they could and had filled all the spaces between with glass after glass of lemonade.

"Are you finished?" asked Aunt Vootch sweetly.

"Yes, Aunt Vootch," said Amy.

"And did I keep my promise?"

They both nodded.

"Good. La la tee dee dum . . . And now I'll keep another promise that I made to *myself*. To teach you discipline! You runaways! Look at this number." She held up a card which read zero.

Joshua said under his breath, "Oh no! The pigpen special."

"You ate like pigs just now," shouted Aunt Vootch. "Now you can live like pigs for a while."

She took Amy and Joshua by their ears and marched them out to the pigpen, opened the gate, and threw them into the mud. Then she took a length of chain and fastened their right wrists to it with old handcuffs she'd bought at a charity auction for sheriffs' widows. She locked the other end of the chain to an iron ring on a big wooden post inside the pen.

Then Aunt Vootch slopped the hogs, throwing a mess of rotten eggs, spoiled tomatoes, and bad cabbages into the pen. Out came the pigs, all three, grunting and squealing. "Eat with them!" she shouted. "They'll teach you manners! You can sleep in the mud with the hogs tonight! You'll think twice before running off to town again, I'll bet a dollar or two on that!" Then she threw in one last cabbage and went back into the house.

The hogs soon fed themselves into sleepiness, and Joshua and Amy were left alone, covered with mud and rotten tomatoes. They sat for a long time without saying a word.

Amy spoke first. "She tricked us. She's tricky-mean, which is the worst mean of all. I don't trust anybody anywhere anymore!"

"You've been saying that for over two years now, ever since Larison's Creek."

"Well, they killed them, didn't they? The cavalrymen! I don't trust anybody!"

"Not even me?" asked Joshua.

"Well . . . maybe you. Sometimes. But no one older than fifteen. Never!"

"You keep that up," said Joshua, "and you'll get as loco as Aunt Vootch."

"Joshua, I can't stand it anymore. I can't! Let's run away. We can go East, to Grandpa and Grandma. They wrote we could come anytime we want."

They had never seen their grandparents, who lived halfway across the continent back in New York City. When their parents had died, Aunt Vootch had written East saying all would be well, for she was opening her heart and home to the children. After that, whenever Amy and Joshua wrote to their grandparents, Aunt Vootch read the letter first to make sure it was full of "heart" and "home" and no complaints.

Joshua thought about Amy's idea of running away for a moment. Then he said, "It'll never work. New York's too far away. And besides, she'll get the sheriff to catch us and bring us back. Then she'll punish us every night for a year."

"You're always scared about everything. You're scared of every kid in school. And now you're scared to run away."

"I am not!" Joshua shouted. "Those kids are always after me, and they're bigger than me and you know it!"

"Well . . ." Amy shook the chain fastened to her handcuff. "We can't get out of this anyway. . . . I wish—I wish we had Ma and Pa back," she said. "Remember when they taught us how to ride? And how Pa would play his harmonica at night? And how Ma always saved the egg money for presents? I keep thinking about them—"

"So do I!" Joshua interrupted. "Stop talking about them! Just stop, okay?" He punched the post with his free fist, even though it hurt. He had to do *something* to keep from crying. He punched it again and noticed that the post moved slightly.

"Amy! Look!" He pulled with all his might, and the fence post moved a little more. "See! It's not quite straight anymore. I'm gonna try to pull it up."

Joshua stood and put his arms around the post, and Amy followed, for they were handcuffed to the chain like a team of horses. When he raised his right arm, Amy had to raise hers. He pushed against the post, then tugged it back, again and again, in the same way that he worked nails back and forth to pull them from boards. And finally it was loose. They pulled together, and the post came up out of the earth with a grinding sound.

"What do we do now?" asked Amy.

"Escape, that's what. Okay? How's that for scared? We're gonna escape from Aunt Vootch! We're going to New York even if it takes a hundred years! But first we have to get Grandpa's address. And our guns. Come on, help me haul the post."

"I hate those guns, Josh! They remind me of Ma and Pa."

"But I need 'em."

"There's no bullets."

"Need 'em anyway. Come on, Amy, let's go!"

They carried the post between them and moved slowly toward the house. A lamp was lit in Aunt Vootch's bedroom.

"*Sssh.* She's going to bed," said Joshua. "Let's go round the other end."

They moved along the edge of the yard to the porch steps. Amy knew every creaky board on the porch, so she took the lead, stepping sideways, then forward, then sideways again, while Joshua tried to step exactly where she stepped.

Amy pressed gently against the front door. "It's latched."

"We can open it," said Joshua. "All I need's my pocketknife. Set the post down a minute." He felt in all his pockets, but the knife was gone. "It must have fallen in the pen. Probably two feet down in the mud by now. You got a big hairpin?"

"I don't use any. I got braids."

"Well, let me see. . . ." He looked around the porch and saw one of Aunt Vootch's number cards lying on the floor. "Hey, look at this. I bet Aunt Vootch is gonna help us escape. Watch."

Joshua took the card and slid it into the crack between the door and the wall, just above the door handle. Then he raised the card slowly, trying to catch the wooden latch on the inside. "I think I've got it." And sure enough, the latch moved up with a click and the door swung open.

They tiptoed through the kitchen, carefully steering the post around the chairs and table. At the entrance to the sitting room they stopped and listened. There wasn't a sound in the house.

"She must've fallen asleep," said Amy.

"*Sssh.* She never sleeps," whispered Joshua. "She walks around in the middle of the night like a witch."

"No, she doesn't. I hear her snore all the time."

They climbed the stairs, still carrying the fence post. Joshua didn't even try to get the keys to the handcuffs, for Aunt Vootch kept them on a cord around her neck, along with her bottle of smelling salts and a whistle.

They held their breath as they passed her room, and prayed that she wouldn't hear them or smell the mixture of rotten eggs and spoiled tomatoes plastered all over them.

They slipped into Joshua's room and shut the door. Joshua took the two silver-plated guns and stuck them in his belt at either side. Next they went to Amy's room and opened the box of letters from their grand-parents. They tore off the address from the top of one of the letters: 328 Fifth Avenue,

New York, N.Y. Then Amy took her sketchbook and pencils from under a loose floorboard where she'd hidden them. They had been a birthday present from her mother, years ago. A present from the egg money.

"Should we take our Sunday clothes?" Amy asked.

"Naa," said Joshua. "We can't get into them with these handcuffs on. And we can't carry them either. We'll just have to smell like hogs and rotten tomatoes."

Holding the post between them, they edged slowly out of the room and went down the stairs one step at a time. "We'll have to find a blacksmith to knock these off and get free," whispered Joshua. "But not until we're a hundred miles from—"

Joshua stopped abruptly and took a step back. For there at the far end of the sitting room, smiling strangely, was Aunt Vootch. Her face was as white as her nightgown.

"We're cooked," said Amy.

Aunt Vootch walked slowly toward them, but she seemed to be looking right through them, as if they weren't there.

Joshua whispered, "She's walking in her sleep. Get out of her way!"

They pressed against the wall as she glided past them toward the stairs. She brushed against the post and stopped. Joshua quickly pulled it away from her.

"Ahhhh uhh," said Aunt Vootch in a hollow voice. Then she started to titter in a way that Amy and Joshua had never heard before. It was more frightening than her usual screaming voice.

They moved backward into the kitchen and past the table, all the while keeping their eyes on Aunt Vootch. Joshua felt behind him for the door handle, found it, and pulled the door open. Then he whispered to Amy, "Run!"

They turned and ran as fast as they could, dragging the post behind. As they raced across the field, they heard the tittering of Aunt Vootch again, from the house.

"She's loco!" cried Amy. "Loco!"

"Keep running! Keep running!" called Joshua. "You think you're so fast, now let's see you really run!"

3. THE WAY TO NEW YORK

The road was full of sudden shadows in the moonlight. As Amy and Joshua passed the scattered farmhouses, dogs started barking, one after another, down the length of the road. But they soon reached the larger fields where the distant houses seemed small as toys, and the dogs fell silent.

Joshua insisted they walk all night, as far as they could, then sleep during the day. But they had to carry the post between them, and their legs and arms ached. They walked more and more slowly, and finally they couldn't go another step.

They dragged the post into a cornfield at the side of the road and lay down to rest for a few minutes. The earth, covered with corn tassels, was as soft as a feather mattress, and they soon fell asleep, their hands and the post linked together.

Suddenly Joshua woke up. Something had disturbed him, something in his sleep. There was a faint tinkling sound off in the distance. He hesitated a moment, then pushed some cornstalks aside and looked down the road. And there, coming toward them, was a horse and wagon, silver-blue in the moonlight. The horse walked with its head down, nodding as it went, and the wagon nodded up and down, too, as it bounced over the ruts. As it drew closer, Joshua could see a man seated up front, sound asleep. On his head was a top hat resting at a tilt. The magician! It was Mortimer Wintergreen!

Joshua yanked on the chain. "Wake up! Amy, quick! Wake up!"

"Huh . . . What?" she said, turning over.

"We've got to get on that wagon. Come on! We can sneak a ride."

The wagon was alongside them now, and it was a curious wagon, indeed. It was covered with canvas like a prairie schooner, but hanging from all the supports were pots, pans, bottles, scissors, bells, harnesses, and dozens of other clinking, jingling objects. And on the side a sign read:

M. WINTERGREEN, ESQ.,
DEALER IN DRY GOODS AND SUNDRIES.
THE BEST IN THE WEST.

As the wagon moved past them, Joshua raised the post to his shoulder and Amy's handcuffed arm followed.

"Now!" whispered Joshua.

With their arms latched together above the post, they ran out to the road and chased after the wagon.

"Come on! Keep going!" called Joshua. "Don't pull the post off my shoulder. Amy, come on!"

As they caught up to the wagon, they could feel the gravel being kicked back at them by the rear wheels. Amy threw her sketchbook in, then reached out, stretching to catch the backboard.

"I . . . I got it!"

She held on to the wagon, and Joshua

pushed her up and in, then heaved the post in after her. He trotted behind, his hand-cuffed arm halfway in, while Amy leaned over and grabbed his shirt and tugged. The shirt ripped, but Amy managed to pull him up, his legs hanging in midair. Then he tumbled over the backboard and fell into the wagon, headfirst.

Amy felt around on the floor and discovered a pile of old clothes. They bunched them into pillows and lay down. The pots and bells and harnesses clinked and jingled, as the wagon shook and bounced along. And within a few minutes, they were asleep once more.

When Joshua woke up the next morning, the sun was already quite high. He yawned and turned over, pulling an old blanket over his head to shut out the light. But . . . he didn't recall finding any blanket last night. Just some old clothes. Joshua rubbed his sore wrist.

The handcuffs were off and the chain was gone! He threw the blanket aside and sat up. *There* were the handcuffs, hanging among some harnesses near the front of the wagon.

And Amy's book was lying right beside her, with her pencils on top. Joshua felt for his guns. They were gone.

"Amy! You're always asleep!" whispered Joshua. "Wake up! We're free! And the wagon's stopped!"

Amy mumbled something and opened her eyes. Around her, above her, in front of her, were a thousand items, half of them broken and wrecked: bottles, tools, books, hats, dishes, curtains, pots, lanterns.

But before she could focus her thoughts, she heard a voice calling, "Flapjack time. Come and get 'em while they last. Flapjacks with huckleberry jam. A flapjack a day keeps the dentist away."

They jumped off the wagon and looked around the side. Mortimer Wintergreen was busily pouring flapjack batter into a sizzling pan over a small fire. "And how are the escaped convicts this morning? I'll be turning you in to the constabulary immediately after breakfast. There's a handsome reward, I'm sure. But I must have my strength. I cannot turn in criminals on an empty stomach. You

look like a dangerous pair. Tarred and to-
matoed, I see."

"We're not convicts," said Joshua in a small,
scared voice. "Can't you tell?"

"Oh, you're not, eh? Then why were you
manacled to a post? And what were you doing
with those six-shooters? Look at yourselves.
You have criminal faces. And I'm sure you
have criminal minds."

"But we're not criminals!" Amy said angrily. How could the man be so dumb? Adults
were either mean or dumb. Or both.

"Haven't I seen you somewhere before? I
can't tell through all that mud. Was it in the
Yankton jail, perchance?"

"I never was in jail! I'm only eleven years
old!" shouted Amy.

"And I'm thirteen," said Joshua. "Remember? You gave me some free Injun
tonic . . . only I left it behind in the barn."

"Free? Impossible. I never give anything
away. Nonetheless, a hundred and six apologies. I thought you were members of the
Danville gang. Very dangerous. Your guns
fooled me. Well, if you're only kids, you can

join me for a bit of breakfast. Naturally, you'll pay when you can. Now get over to that creek there and wash up. From head to fingernails. I'll keep the flapjacks flapping."

Amy and Joshua washed as fast as they could, trying to get all the mud and tomato off. It felt good to be clean again. As they hurried back, they saw that Wintergreen had set out a little table for three, complete with a tiny vase holding a pink wildflower.

"Must retain some semblance of civilization," said Wintergreen. "I never dine without napkins and flowers. And, if possible, a choice wine." Then Wintergreen looked at Amy and Joshua carefully. "Ah ha," he said. "Clean faces. Say! Now I know where I've seen you before! Couldn't tell with all that mud and tomato paste. You came to my show yesterday. Very embarrassing. Skunks and clotheslines. Bad for business. People tend to want their money back. By the way, just for the record, what might your names happen to be?"

"Amy Baines."

"Joshua Baines."

"Pleased to meet. Name's Mortimer Q.

Wintergreen. Now have some of that huckleberry jam. Don't tickle it with a touch here and there. Slap it on. The jam and flapjacks must become acquainted."

"Can I have my guns back, Mr. Wintergreen?" Joshua asked. "I need 'em."

"Ah yes. The artillery. Your guns are on the front seat up there. You can have them back directly after breakfast. Now, if I'm not being too inquisitive, tell me something, friends. Just how did you two manage to get chained like that?"

Joshua chewed quickly and swallowed. "Do you know my aunt Vootch, Mr. Wintergreen, sir?"

"What's all this mister and sir business? Just call me Mortimer. Or else I'll call you Master Joshua and you Mistress Amy. If we do that, we'll never get to pass the pepper. . . . Now let me think. Your aunt Vootch? Vootch. Vootch. Rhymes with *pooch*, *smooch*, and *brooch*. Little memory system I have . . . No, I can't say I've ever met the lady."

"She's no lady," said Amy. "She's rotten. *She* chained us to the post."

"Ah. Well, well. Stern aunt. Sad. But it isn't as if she whipped you."

"She sure did whip us," said Joshua. "She's crazy. She whips everybody in sight when she's on the warpath."

"By Thomas Quincy Jefferson!" said Wintergreen. "I got whipped by a lady just yesterday, exiting rapidly from a barn."

"That was her."

"Why, that woman has the arm of a lumberjack. You two are lucky you're still alive."

"That's why we ran away."

"Runaways, eh? Tell me the whole gruesome story, children. An inch at a time. Space it between flapjack munchings. Proceed."

Joshua told Mortimer everything, from the Battle of Larison's Creek to the previous night when they'd dragged themselves into the wagon. By the time they'd finished, Mortimer had poured milk for them and put out gingerbread cookies.

"Frightening, frightening," said Mortimer. "She's probably after you right now. We'd better get going. I'll put away this table. You throw these chairs in the back and swing up onto the front seat with me. Take those cookies with you. And grab your guns!"

Within a few minutes, they were packed and ready. "Gee yap, Chrysanthemum! Gee yap," Mortimer called. The horse nodded several times, then with a jolt the wagon was on its way.

As they rode along, Joshua rubbed his wrist. It was red and bruised from the handcuff. "Mr. Wintergreen—I mean Mortimer—could you tell us how you got those handcuffs off?"

Mortimer felt behind him, in the wagon, and brought out an enormous ring of keys. There were hundreds, of every size and shape.

"Finest collection in the West," said Mortimer. "It's growing day by day. Got your handcuffs open on the eighteenth try."

Amy had wanted to ask Mortimer a question all morning. "Mr. Mortimer, how did you—you know, in the barn yesterday—how were you able to pull that lady's clothesline out of your hat?"

"Curiosity killed the canary," said Mortimer. "Magicians never reveal their secrets. Any other questions, my fine-furred friends?"

"Well . . ." said Joshua. "Whereabouts are you heading?"

"I'm going east," said Mortimer. "To civilization. To high culture. To riches. Away from cornfields and prairies and barn shows. I'm returning to the great city of New York City, where money flows like pickle juice. Where I can make my mark upon the legitimate stage as the world's most stupendous and highly paid magician."

"We're heading there, too!" said Amy. "Away from cornfields and pigpens and Aunt Vootch. Grandpa and Grandma live there. Didn't we tell you? Show him their address, Josh. Can we go with you, Mr. Mortimer?"

"Certainly," said Mortimer, as he studied Joshua's letter. "Three twenty-eight Fifth Avenue? Excellent address. Wealthy part of town. Go east, by all means, young lady. Go east!"

"But you're driving toward the west," said Joshua.

"Nonsense. East is straight ahead. Always

remember: The sun rises in the west. . . . I wonder if your grandpapa might not reimburse me for my many sundry expenses in delivering you to his door. . . ."

"But Mr. Mortimer, the sun rises in the *east*," said Amy.

"Tush, tush, young lady. Leave the astronomy to us elders. . . . Anyone with a Fifth Avenue address is certain to pay generously, don't you think?"

"But east is back there," said Joshua, pointing. "Toward that dust cloud in the distance."

Mortimer turned and looked. "That dust is to the west. Christopher Q. Columbus! Someone's riding at a rapid pace, raising dust like that. It may be Indians! Come on, Chrysanthemum. Gee yap!" The wagon sped ahead, jolting and shaking, while all the pots and pans and bottles and bells made a racket that would have frightened a herd of cattle into stampeding.

"Injuns are okay," said Amy. "It's the cavalry you gotta look out for!"

"That's not Injuns," called Joshua over the

noise. "Look! It's Orion pulling Aunt Vootch's buggy. We're sunk!"

"It is!" shouted Amy. "And she's hung one of her cards up on a pole!"

"Oh cucumbers! Cucumbers!" Mortimer shouted. "She's gaining on us! Gee yap, Chrysanthemum! Gee yap!"

4. THE MAGIC HAT

The sound of Orion's hoofbeats grew louder and louder, as Aunt Vootch's light buggy sped closer to their heavy, rumbling wagon.

"What manner of horse does that woman possess?" asked Mortimer. "It's making my Chrysanthemum look like a sick pussycat."

"Orion's a mighty big horse," Joshua said.

"And a mighty mean one," added Amy. "He's as rotten as Aunt Vootch."

"Ah well. Chrysanthemum may be old and slow, but she's a kindly horse. A great one for nuzzling. But right now it's time for drastic action! Here, young man! Take hold of the reins!"

After giving the reins to Joshua, Mortimer took his hat off and placed it carefully in his lap. He looked back once more toward Aunt Vootch's buggy, then slowly moved his hand down into his hat.

"Well, well. What have we here?" Out came his hand, holding a large Idaho potato. He tossed it into the back of the wagon. "Excellent baked with a bit of melted pork fat. Waste not, want not. Let's try once more." And again he put his hand into his hat. This time he pulled out a broken roof shingle. "Oh, mucilage!" called Mortimer, tossing the shingle into the road. "That's not worth a bent nail."

Amy didn't know what to make of it. It certainly was skillful, but why was he doing tricks at a time like this? Joshua could barely control the horse and wagon as they hurtled along. Was the man plain crazy?

"She's gaining on us!" shouted Amy. "Mr. Mortimer, *do* something!"

"Calmly, calmly," said Mortimer. "We're working on it. Patience at all costs. If you don't fail at first, try, try again." Then he reached into the hat and pulled out a beautiful pink teacup decorated with yellow flowers. "My, my. Worth at least twenty cents.

We'll put this in our household department."
And he leaned back and put the cup into a
basket behind the seat.

Then suddenly, they heard the voice of
Aunt Vootch crackling toward them. "I have
you now, you runaways! And you, Wintergreen! I know who you are! You'll hang for
kidnaping! I'll have your head!"

As the buggy pulled alongside their wagon,
they could see Aunt Vootch leaning toward
them. Her hair blew behind like Orion's
streaming mane, and her eyes were as sharp
as thistles. One of her cards was fastened to
her buggy; it bore a number Amy had never
seen before: 131,313.

"I'll fix you now!" shouted Aunt Vootch.
As they raced along, side by side, she swung
the buggy whip at them, hitting Mortimer
across his head.

"I've been lashed again!" cried Mortimer.
"Your aunt ought to be a lion tamer!"

The whip came down once more, barely
missing Amy. "Under the seat, girl!" called
Mortimer. "That whip has the sting of a
rattlesnake."

Amy scrambled under the wooden seat and

looked out. Aunt Vootch was standing in her buggy, poised to strike like a hawk above its prey. Down snapped the whip across Mortimer's arms.

"Desist, woman!" he shouted. "I'm not your horse! I'm Mortimer Wintergreen, and you're making an enemy of me *and* my hat! You have been warned, madam!"

Mortimer hurriedly dipped down into the hat again and pulled out a bunch of radishes. "Excellent for salad. Worth at least three cents. Patience! Patience!" He threw the radishes over his shoulder, into the rear of the wagon, then put his hand down into his hat, again. This time he brought out several long black leather straps. "Ah ha!" said Mortimer. "Success, at last, I do believe."

At that same instant, Orion bolted free from Aunt Vootch's buggy and galloped off the road and across a wheat field. Her buggy immediately slowed and fell behind. The whip came sizzling down again, only to strike the backboard of Mortimer's wagon.

Amy and Joshua saw it all, but it took them a few seconds to realize what had happened. Amy picked up one of the leather straps and shouted, "Joshua! Look! It's Aunt Vootch's harness! Look!"

From behind Mortimer's wagon, Aunt Vootch screamed, "Bandits! Thieves! You've stolen my harness! I'll get you! I'll get you all!"

Amy turned back, but Aunt Vootch and her buggy had disappeared in the dust from Mortimer's wagon. Then faintly, from a distance, they heard her call once more: "I'llll . . . ge-e-e-t . . . you-u-u! . . ."

At last Mortimer slowed Chrysanthemum down and let her ease off to a halt. He gave her a little water, then continued at a slower pace. "Good girl. You almost won the race, but you had too much of a load. No, no. Don't be discouraged. You did well. For supper tonight you can have baked Idaho potato with radishes au gratin."

Amy and Joshua were still dumbfounded by the incredible harness trick. "How did you do it?" asked Joshua. "I thought for sure we were cooked and ready to be carved."

"Ah, well, well, well," said Mortimer. "Sometimes the hat is in a better mood than other times. It's all a matter of mood. . . . Say, that's a good harness. I'd sell it, except she'd be sure to accuse me of robbery as well as kidnaping, and I'd hang twice in the same day. And that, friends, takes a very strong neck."

"But how *did* you do it?" Amy asked, picking up the harness. "You can tell us. We're real expert at keeping secrets. That's 'cause we've had to keep secrets from Aunt Vootch all the time. Is the trick very hard to do?"

"Trick? What trick? You're under a vast misconception. This isn't a trick hat. This is an authentic bona fide magic hat. Watch. One puts one hand in thusly. One wiggles one's fingers a trifle. One feels hither and yon. And one grasps whatsoever is there. Like this." He pulled out an old torn copy of a newspaper called *Harper's Weekly, A Journal of Civilization.*

"Well, well," said Mortimer. "Civilization, eh? Very uplifting. I'll read it after dinner." He tossed the paper into the back of the wagon. "See what I mean? Magic."

"You mean there's no trick things that you do?" asked Joshua.

"None at all," Mortimer answered. "It's

pure, simple, everyday, run-of-the-mill magic."

"Would I be able to do it?" asked Joshua. A magic hat! If only he had a hat like that, no one would ever dare bother him again, no matter how big they were. "Can I try?" he asked.

"Perish the thought!" said Mortimer. "Dangerous. In fact, it could be fatal. This is a very temperamental hat. I traveled in a circus one summer, and the trapeze artist stole the hat. Thought he could get gold out of it. . . . If this was a gold-giving hat, I wouldn't have had to work in that circus. . . . Poor fellow. He took the hat into his tent and pulled out a ravenously starved tiger. The roars and screams could be heard clear to the next town. And from then on, all he was able to do was sell candy apples. . . . With his left hand, of course. Now if you'd like to try your luck, go ahead. But please do it over by that hill yonder, not near us."

Mortimer held the hat out to Amy, but she pulled her hand back. Then he plunked his hat back on his head. "Wise girl," he said. "You're smarter than the trapeze artist and you're only seven years old."

"Eleven," said Amy.

"Ah yes, eleven it is. Now why don't you two climb in the back of the wagon and play a game of checkers. There's a board on the second shelf. The pieces are from seventeen different sets, but they're all good solid wood. And remember, every minute you play, you're heading farther east. We'll be in Iowa before you can say, 'Peter Piper picked out a plum eating his curds and whey.' "

Joshua and Amy climbed over the seat into the covered part of the wagon. "Look at all those parasols," said Amy, searching for the checkers set. "There's eight—no, nine of 'em."

"And how about these!" Joshua pointed to a row of hats stacked one on top of the other. "I'll bet they're all magic." He took one and turned it over.

"Don't touch it!" Amy whispered.

But Joshua had already put his hand into it. "Nothing," he said. Then he tried all the other hats, one by one. "Guess he's got the only good one. But I'm gonna try his, you bet your boots."

"No!" said Amy. "You could get killed. He might have a tiger waiting inside there for you."

"Now look who's scared. I *need* a hat like that. It's better than these guns we got. Anyway, I don't believe that story about the tiger. Mr. Mortimer's all kind of backward and upside down."

"I know," said Amy. "That's why I don't trust him. Or his hat."

"Yeah, but you don't trust anybody. . . . Okay, come on. Let's just play checkers."

"I don't feel like playing. . . . Josh, we oughta jump off the wagon. Mr. Mortimer, maybe, is just as crazy as Aunt Vootch."

"We can't! We'd die of thirst out here. Besides, we're heading right toward the Badlands. That's where the bandits have their hideouts. In caves and on the mesas. Every gang in South Dakota has a hideout there. 'Cause there's no sheriffs or cavalry or anything. If we don't die of thirst, we'll get shot!"

"There you go again! Scared! Don't you

remember Pa told us they called it the Bad-lands only 'cause you can't farm there, the land's so bad? Besides, the Badlands are on the other side of the Missouri River!"

"So what? We're still heading there! And Pa *did* say there were bandits! And Injuns! So we better stay on the wagon. At least that way we got Mr. Mortimer and his hat, and maybe that's better than the sheriff or the cavalry. He doesn't know which way is east, but he sure knew how to stop Aunt Vootch."

5. GREENERWINTS AND WINTERMINTS

As the wagon rattled and jangled along, Mortimer whistled song after song. "Whistling soothes the soul on the long stretches of the prairie!" Mortimer shouted to them in the back of the wagon. "Almost as good as owning a piano!"

Amy and Joshua tried playing checkers, but every time the wagon lurched badly, the pieces slid all over the board. They finally gave up. Amy took her book of blank sheets down from a shelf and started sketching the bells and bottles and harnesses hanging in the wagon. She had to steady her hand as the wagon bounced, but she soon filled a page with her clear, careful drawings.

"That's pretty good," said Joshua. "Too

bad you don't draw people no more. You drew them real good. Even Ma said so. Why don't you draw a picture of Mr. Mortimer? It'd be better than all those bells and stuff."

"You keep telling me to draw people! Well, I hate people! You get Ma and Pa back first!"

"Well, that's loco. I can't get 'em back."

"And I won't draw anybody!"

"Okay," said Joshua. "Do whatever you want." He turned and crawled to the opening at the back of the wagon to see where they were. The dirt was blowing off the rear wheels like the wake of a ship.

Joshua pointed toward the ground. "Amy, look! No more road. There's just grass and scrub. We're out on the open prairie. And it'll get drier and drier and full of gorges and cliffs and that's the Badlands."

"Well, if it is, don't you think Mr. Mortimer can tell?"

"I think maybe we'd better help him figure it out," said Joshua.

They crawled to the front and saw Mortimer sitting with his head on one shoulder, sound asleep. Chrysanthemum plodded on slowly, half asleep herself.

"Should we wake him?" asked Amy.

"Mr. Wintergreen," Joshua said softly.

"Mmmfh," Mortimer muttered in his sleep. "Smother it with mushrooms and onions, waiter. And remember, I like my steak rare. . . . Mmfh perfumph . . ."

"Mr. Wintergreen . . ."

"Umf . . . A little whiskey and soda, did you say? Impossible! I never touch anything stronger than orange juice. . . ."

"*Mr. Wintergreen!*"

"Hark, hark. Music with dinner. Delightful . . . Umpfh . . . I would like to request the Blue Danube Waltz. . . . Mmfh . . ."

"MR. WINTERGREEN!" Amy and Joshua screamed together.

"Mmumfh . . . The violins are as sweet as Vermont maple syrup. Ah m'lady, what a romantic evening. A Strauss Waltz, a steak with onions and thou . . . Mmfh . . ."

"He's dead to the world. Now's my chance!" Joshua reached for Mortimer's top hat.

"Stupid!" called Amy. "Don't touch it!"

But Joshua had the brim in his hand. He

raised the hat an inch or so, ready to jump if anything should happen. Suddenly Mortimer sat bolt upright.

"Police!" he called out, as Joshua pulled his hand back. "Robbers! Murderers! Assassins!" Mortimer shouted.

He turned in confusion from Joshua to Amy. "Wha . . . what happened? I must have been dreaming. . . . Strange, I dreamed I was in a grand restaurant in the great city of New York City having a spot of steak and Strauss, when suddenly the violinist stole my top hat. Very distressing. You go to a quality place and that's what happens. Man's got to watch his hat, coat, and canary these days. . . . By the by, where has Chrysanthemum been taking us?"

"We're out on the open prairie," said Joshua. "Heading *west*."

"You mean east," said Mortimer. "Soon we'll see the fields of Iowa. Golden grains as far as you can whistle. By Patrick Quincy Henry, dreaming about steak has made me hungry. My stomach is sending messages to my brain. It's saying we ought to have an early supper today. And I agree."

Mortimer stopped the wagon and fed and watered Chrysanthemum. Then he gathered some brush for a fire.

"Our menu will be flapjacks with huckleberry jam and radishes. I regret to say that my hat has not been in the best of moods lately. Overworked. It never gives its best when it's overworked. Broken shingles. Old newspapers. Radishes. It needs a rest. If only we had a farm nearby, I could trade a parasol for a pork chop."

"But we love flapjacks," said Amy.

"Brave girl," Mortimer murmured as he started the fire. "But wait till the hat gives us a solid week of stale spinach, as it did last month." He threw more brush on the fire and stood back. "Ah," he said. "Let us enjoy this glorious blaze a bit, before dinner. I feel a spell of profound laziness nipping at my toes."

As they sat around the fire, Amy studied Mortimer Wintergreen's face and wondered how difficult it would be to draw him. His mustache was too thin, his ears were too big, and his chin seemed too chubby. And for all his light talk and chatter, his mouth, somehow, looked sad. Would he be offended if someone drew him as he really was? Well, it didn't matter. She wasn't going to sketch him. Or anyone.

"Mr. Mortimer," Joshua asked, throwing a stray piece of brush into the fire, "did you always own that hat?"

"Ah, not at all. This hat is not popular. No. It travels from head to head. I bought it some years ago for two silver dollars from a ship's captain at a New York dock. The hat had caused him no end of trouble at sea. I understand the mainsail came out of the hat one breezy day, in one long endless ribbon. Terrible for navigation. That captain, in turn, had bought it from a very proper gentleman in Burma. The gentleman pulled his own trousers out of the hat, right smack in the middle of a lavish dinner party. Most embarrassing. His undershorts, I am told, were bright pink. As was his face. Yes indeed, this is a very temperamental hat. At times vicious."

"Then why don't you sell it?" asked Joshua.

"A simple reason. It is after all, despite its stubborn streak, a true magic hat. And I intend to let it help me become the world's foremost magician. If only I'd had this hat forty years ago. Yes. . . . Back then, I saw my dear pater and mater—that's father and mother to you—I saw them struggle for years and years with their little traveling act. At the ripe old age of three, I became part of the team. The Dancing Wintergreens. I've gained a bit of weight since then, but I was light on my feet in those golden, miserable days. Ah, the memories. After some re- sounding setbacks, the Dancing Winter- greens became the Singing Greenwinters. That didn't work either. Then we tried a bit of acrobatics. We became the Balancing Greenerwints. Several more years and sev- eral broken arms brought us to our final des- tination: the Magic Wintermints. That's how I first learned magic. I mean make-believe magic, not magic-hat magic. I was sawed in half two thousand six hundred and fifty-two times, in every state of this noble Union, as well as Canada. We made enough money to eat and to buy a few necessities such as shoes and soap. But my poor mater and pater died broke and brokenhearted. And that, my friends, is why I want to keep this hat, nasty and brutish though it can be, and become the greatest magician in the history of the universe."

"But I *like* your hat," said Amy. "In fact— maybe—I'd like to draw a picture of it. Can I, Mr. Mortimer?"

"Certainly. So long as you stay your distance."

Amy rushed over to the wagon to get her book and pencils. "She won't draw pictures of people anymore," Joshua said to Mortimer. "Since Ma and Pa got killed, she won't. She could draw people really, really good."

"Aha. Well, well . . . A form of grieving, no doubt. Ever since my dear mater and pater passed to the great beyond, I have refused to permit myself to be sawn in half."

As Mortimer set out the table and chairs for dinner, Amy followed him with her book, sketching his hat from all angles.

"Please, Mr. Mortimer! Don't move for a minute!"

"Ah yes. Try the other side. That's my hat's good side. Less battered there."

Soon Amy's sketches were finished. She

studied them, made a few corrections, then held her book open high above her head, toward Mortimer.

"Nice pictures," said Mortimer. "Very skillful, I do confess. But what are you doing, might I ask? Giving your book an airing?"

"No. I'm showing the drawings to the hat."

"Show it a picture of some steak and baked potato," said Mortimer. "Maybe it will get the hint. . . . What was *that*!"

"What was what?" asked Joshua.

"Something just fell down from the hat onto my head. I fear to look."

Mortimer lifted the hat gingerly and felt the top of his head with the tips of his fingers. He grasped a small object, looked at it, then held it out to Amy.

"Well, well, my lucky lass. It's a present for you, no doubt. An orange crayon. My hat must like you. Here, take it."

"Oh, thank you, Mr. Mortimer."

"Not me. Thank my hat."

"Oh . . . uh, thank you, Hat."

"You're perfectly welcome," said Mortimer. "Now let's eat."

6. TAFFY

Just then, Joshua saw a thin line of dust in the distance, and two men on horseback, dark against the sun. "Look! Over to the west! Cavalrymen!"

"To the east. Pony Express riders," said Mortimer.

Joshua shaded his eyes with his hand. "They're heading toward us. Well, at least it ain't Aunt Vootch."

"I'll set the table for five," said Mortimer, and he immediately put out more plates and forks. "We need a flower for the table. Amy, my lass, find us a little posy or two or three."

While Joshua helped Mortimer with the fire, Amy searched among the wild grass and brought back some small yellow flowers.

Mortimer began pouring the flapjack batter, while Amy arranged and rearranged the flowers in the vase. "Ah, you needn't fuss at all, at all," he said. "They look just fine. In fact, I may eat one for an appetizer. Quite tasty when you're out of lettuce."

Then the riders were suddenly upon them, thundering over a nearby rise. The men were unshaven and their clothes were covered with dirt.

"Well looka here, Roscoe," said the taller man. "A picnic in the middle of the prairie."

"Pass me the pickles, Thad," the other jeered.

"A splendid good evening to you," said Mortimer as the two men dismounted. "Yes indeed."

"Okay, reach!" Roscoe pulled out a six-shooter from his holster. "Get 'em up! All of you! Up!"

Though he could scarcely move from fright, Joshua still managed to whisper to Amy, "See. I told you. Bandits."

Mortimer raised his hands. "The flapjacks will be ruined. I've got to flap the flipjacks! I mean flip the flapjacks!"

"I hate flapjacks!" Roscoe aimed his gun at the pancakes and fired twice. The sharp *crack crack* of the gun was followed by the whine of a ricocheting bullet: *bi-weeeeng.*

"Leave them flapjacks alone!" shouted Thad. "That's our supper, you dumb coyote!" Then he stepped over to the pan, still covering Mortimer and the children with his gun. He scooped up chunks of flapjack with his hand and shoved the half-cooked batter into his mouth.

"My dear visitors," said Mortimer. "You will note that we've already set out extra plates for you. You can put away your guns. We're as harmless as bluebirds in a butter churn."

"Yeah? What's that kid got stuck in his belt? Lollipops?" asked Thad as he pushed more batter into his mouth.

"But—but these guns aren't even loaded," said Joshua. "Th-they just got engravings on them, on the silver plating, for show."

"Silver plated, eh? We can sell 'em in Sioux Falls. Okay, Roscoe, get his guns."

"I don't take no orders from you, Thad," Roscoe said angrily.

"You ain't got enough horse sense to do anything *but* take orders. Shooting at flap-jacks! Okay, I'll get the guns. But keep them covered!"

Thad took Joshua's guns and tossed them into the wagon. "Beat-up horse," he said. "Beat-up wagon. Lots of junk in it though. Yeah, we can sell it all in Sioux Falls. Hey, looka there, Roscoe. He's even got parasols."

"Where?" Roscoe asked, looking toward the wagon.

Thad reached in and pulled out a parasol. "See that! The latest style, hey boy?" Then he opened it and twirled it.

"I hate parasols!" said Roscoe. "The gals who carry 'em, they all got fancy manners. They're the kind that think I'm a pig." And he suddenly spun around and shot at the parasol, ripping it to shreds: *Crack! Crack! Crack! Crack!*

"You ain't no pig, Roscoe," said Thad, throwing the parasol away. "No sirree."

"You bet I ain't."

"You're a pebble-brained donkey!"

"You watch what you call me!" Roscoe aimed his gun at Thad. "You watch!"

"Better reload that there six-shooter first, Roscoe. It's fresh outta bullets. You just killed a parasol and some flapjacks."

Thad scooped up the last of the flapjacks and crammed it into his mouth. He chewed for a moment and swallowed. Then his face turned red as he started to choke. "Aggh! Aggh!" he called.

"What? What's the matter? Thad, what's the matter?" Roscoe asked.

"Agghh! Gachh! Glochh!" Thad held on to the wagon, sputtering and gasping. Then he turned toward Roscoe, who was busily reloading his gun, and gave a twisted half smile.

"What's the matter, Thad?" asked Roscoe nervously.

"*What's the matter, Thad?* I swallowed your bullet, that's what, cricket brain!"

"Oh . . . That's okay. You don't have to worry none, Thad. It was a clean bullet. Real clean. Right from the box. Never been in my belt at all."

"Ah me," said Mortimer, his hands still raised above his head. "It would have been better with huckleberry jam. A great pity. Yes."

Thad turned to Mortimer. "You don't talk, mister; you listen! We're gonna be heading along, now. Roscoe there, he's gonna drive your wagon. Right, Roscoe? Don't worry, we'll send someone to get you, on our way to Sioux Falls. I don't let kids starve t' death out on the prairie. Me, I got scruples."

"I hate kids." Roscoe pointed his gun at Amy. "Hate 'em!"

Very calmly, as if he were ignoring Roscoe, Mortimer whispered loudly to Joshua, "Don't worry, m'boy. Let them take the wagon. Your grandpapa's gold is safe in my hat."

Roscoe lowered his gun slightly. "What gold?"

"Beg pardon?" said Mortimer. "I don't catch your meaning. It isn't cold out at all. Very pleasant, for July, if it doesn't start to precipitate."

"Give me that hat!" Roscoe growled.

"Ah me. All is lost, Joshua. But never fear, lad. Your grandpapa's tough. He can live on snake meat and fried grasshoppers, if he must."

Mortimer held his hat out toward Roscoe. "Go ahead. Take the gold. But let me keep my hat. It's the only headgear I possess."

"*I'll* take the gold," said Thad, pushing Roscoe aside. "You keep them covered, horseshoe head."

Thad slipped his hand into the hat still held by Mortimer and brought out a thick, sticky rope of soft taffy. He tried to shake it loose, but more poured out, covering his arms to the elbows.

"I believe my hat's hit the jackpot on the first try, this time," said Mortimer. "Your drawing helped put it in a good mood, young lady. Well, well."

Thad grabbed the candy with both hands and tried to free himself, but it was hopeless. The taffy stuck to everything in its path. And Mortimer carefully tilted his hat to help it flow even faster.

"Roscoe! Get this dad-blamed stuff offa me. Get it off!"

"I *hate* taffy!" said Roscoe, aiming his gun at the thick flow. *Crack! Crack!*

"Don't shoot the taffy! You'll hit *me!*"

shouted Thad. "Bucket brain! Shoot the hat! Shoot the *hat*!"

Crack! Crack! Crack! Three bullets cut right through the hat, but Mortimer still held it firmly. And the taffy continued to flow.

"Help me! It won't stop! Roscoe! Help me!" called Thad.

Roscoe tried to scrape the taffy from Thad's arms, but it twined around his own wrists. "I'm caught, too!" Roscoe shouted.

"No you ain't!" said Thad. "Turn. Turn around and pull!"

Roscoe twisted and tugged, but it only managed to trap him further. His gun slipped from his hand and fell into the sticky mound rising around his feet.

Soon strands of taffy hung from their arms and legs like a limp spider web. More and more poured out of the hat, like lava from an erupting volcano. The outlaws strained and grunted, but they could move only in slow motion, stretching the thick strands of taffy like giant rubber bands.

Mortimer plucked the outlaws' guns out of the candy and threw them into the wagon.

"There we are," he said, as he tapped the hat to help the last of the taffy flow out. "Dessert, my fine-feathered felons. You can eat your way to freedom." Mortimer took two spoons from the table and stuck them right under each outlaw's chin. "But don't worry, I'll send someone from the next town to get you. Like the sheriff and a posse. I don't let outlaws die from eating too much taffy out on the prairie. I've got scruples." And Mortimer clapped his hat back onto his head.

The bandits tried to shout, but all that emerged were some huge taffy bubbles, for the candy had risen almost to their noses.

"All right, my friends," said Mortimer. "Let's pile the table and chairs into the wagon and be on our way. But I think I'll take a little dish of dessert with us. In exchange for the flapjacks."

He scooped up some taffy with a coffee scoop, then joined Amy and Joshua on the wagon. "Gee yap, Chrysanthemum. Let's shake the dust from yonder scoundrels."

Mortimer tried to raise his hat to bid the bandits farewell, but it wouldn't budge. "By Benjamin Quincy Franklin! My hat's stuck to my head! It's the taffy! I'll have to work it loose, tonight, with boiling water. Very embarrassing. . . . Well, well. It's time to head east. Gee yap, Chrysanthemum! Gee yap!"

And to Amy and Joshua's surprise, Mortimer made a wide turn with the wagon and started heading in the right direction at last, away from the setting sun.

7. HATS, HANDCUFFS, AND HEALTH TONIC

lthough Amy and Joshua nibbled on the taffy as they rode along, they were hungry for a real dinner, for corn and chicken and steaming-hot rolls with balls of fresh butter. But there wasn't any food left, not even flapjack batter. Amy asked Mortimer if he could try the hat again for some supper, but he told her the taffy had strained it to the breaking point, and it needed a night of rest.

They rode along silently, listening to the clinking bells and bottles ring with a strange Oriental music on the darkening prairie. Amy sketched Chrysanthemum's lowered head and spindly back on a blank sheet in her book.

As the sun slipped below some low hills behind them, Mortimer finally said, "It's time to make a public statement. It seems from all evidence that the sun sets in the west. Those outlaws were headed for Sioux Falls, and Sioux Falls is to the east. You were correct in all particulars. We were heading for Japan. My apologies. Tush, tush, don't say a word. An apology in time saves nine. . . . And now, my friends, we ought to stop for the night. I have to boil some water to loosen the taffy, and then I'll repair the bullet holes in my chapeau."

"What's a chapeau?" asked Amy.

"A chapeau is a hat. I see I shall have to teach you a dash of French as we go. Also a little Greek, a touch of higher mathematics, and a *soupçon* of poetry. So that when we reach New York, you two will be thoroughly civilized human personages."

"What's a *soup's on?*" asked Joshua. "It sounds like the soup's ready. And I sure wish it was. I'm hungry."

"*Soupçon* is a French word meaning a small amount. Like a pinch of salt. Or a smidge of spicy pepper . . . By Balboa, I'm hungry, too. Ah me. If we can survive till morning, maybe my hat will lay a fresh egg or two. . . . Whoa, Chrysanthemum. Whoa, girl."

Mortimer set up their camp for the night and, after building a fire, arranged some blankets for Amy and Joshua in the back of the wagon. "Try to get to sleep now," he said. "That way, you won't feel as hungry. I'm about to perform a delicate surgical operation on my taffy-coated noggin. Should you hear any screams, fear not. It's only myself being boiled to a turn. Good night children. Dream about New York and your grandpa and grandma and their great wealth, or some facsimile thereof."

Amy and Joshua got under the blankets and tried not to think about food. Instead, they listened to Mortimer at the side of the wagon, busily working on his hat. Every so often he would let out a yell; then he would whisper to himself, "*Ssh, ssh.* Sleeping children. Keep your big mouth shut, Wintergreen. You're creating a public nuisance."

Amy yawned and asked Joshua, "What's a facsimile?"

"I don't rightly know," he answered.

"He uses all kinds of crazy words. . . .

Joshua, what do you think Grandma and Grandpa are like? You think they're really rich, like Mr. Mortimer says?"

"Don't rightly know."

"You don't rightly know anything!" Amy said, pushing her head down on the blanket.

"Yipe!" called Mortimer. "Yiii! . . . *Ssh. Ssh.* Silence, Wintergreen. Silence."

"I know what," said Amy. "I bet they own a huge restaurant like the one Mr. Mortimer was dreaming about. And we'll be able to eat all the fried chicken and huckleberry pie and—"

"Stop!" said Joshua. "That's making my stomach ache, 'cause I'm as hungry as two horses."

"Me too," said Amy. "Well, maybe they own a big old bank somewhere and count money all day. I think Mr. Mortimer would like that. Good night, Josh."

"G'night."

They both turned over and fell asleep.

When Joshua woke up the next morning, the sun was just edging above the horizon. Strips of red clouds in the distance made him think of bacon. His stomach growled with hunger.

Then he heard Amy's voice at the side of the wagon. "These are done, Mr. Mortimer. Should I take them out of the pan?" There was a sizzling, splattering sound. Joshua jumped off the back of the wagon to look. It *was* bacon!

"You're the one who slept late today," Amy said. "I got up before sunrise. Look!"

The pan was full of bacon curling and crisping beautifully. In a platter on the table, more bacon was heaped with bread and butter and fried potatoes.

"And look at this," said Amy. She held up another crayon, a red one. "It's from the hat. For me."

"Yes indeed," said Mortimer. "We were about to wake you. My hat's in a splendid mood. Undoubtedly it has found a friend, namely you, young lady. And now it's given us enough bacon for a royal feast. But let us not stand here chitter-chattering, friends. Let's attack the victuals."

Joshua and Amy each had three helpings and Mortimer had four. "This bacon's as sweet as honey," said Mortimer. "And the butter's as fresh as a banjo. However, and nevertheless, we must push on to the nearest town. I have to do a little trading. I need some hard cash to purchase the goods my hat has failed to furnish. We're out of coffee, eggs, cookies, and other sundries too numerous to mention."

"And milk," said Amy.

"And milk. Furthermore, we ought to send someone for those two prairie pirates before they manage to eat their way to freedom. So let us ply our way eastward with stout hearts and buoyant brains. Last one in the wagon's a rotten pimento."

Within a few minutes they'd packed everything and were on their way. Chrysanthemum, fresh from a night's rest, stepped along briskly. And before the morning was over, they arrived at a small town.

Mortimer stopped in front of the sheriff's office and went in, leaving Joshua in charge of the wagon. Within a minute, the sheriff raced out of the office with two of his deputies. All three men leaped onto their horses and headed toward the west. Then Mortimer

Wintergreen stepped out of the office, smoking a long thin cigar. He climbed back onto the wagon and ceremoniously flicked the cigar ash off the side.

"Well, friends," said Mortimer, "it looks like we've captured two members of the Clinton gang. Wanted in three states for armed robbery, murder, and shooting parasols on Sunday. The sheriff presented me with this cigar as a token of his esteem. He, of course, will pick up the reward for himself, the swindler. Pardon me, mustn't disillusion youngsters. All sheriffs are honest and all chicken soup contains chicken. Now then. This is an excellent time to sell a little of my all-season hair tonic—"

"I thought it was *health* tonic," Joshua interrupted.

"Ah, so it is. Cures mumps, whooping cough, and hiccups. Now, while the sheriff and his crew are away, we'll just sell a few bottles along with some of the knicker-knacks on the wagon."

Mortimer rolled down the canvas sides of the wagon so everything inside could be seen. Then he stood on the seat and called out,

"Ladies and gentlemen, girls and boys, cats and dogs! May I have your kindliest attention! We are about to begin a sale of the most stupendous collection of home goods, hardware, and health aids in the entire West."

A small crowd had gathered to look at the strange wagon. As Mortimer spoke, others joined them until almost every person on the main street stood watching.

"Yes indeed, friends," Mortimer continued, "and with every purchase, no matter how small, you will receive one, count them, one free bottle of Wintergreen's All-Season Health Tonic, good for the liver, the stomach, and the brain. Guaranteed to cure a total of one hundred and eighteen diseases of humankind, twenty-three of horses, seventeen of dogs, twelve of cats, and twenty-nine of cattle. It will also grow hair on your head and bring forth an abundance of wool on any breed of sheep. Useful too as a light oil for any small machinery on the farm or in the home. And as a special bonus, it may be used to create eleven different salad dressings, including the famous Wintergreen Salad Dressing Française, recipes two cents extra.

And remember, gents and ladies, that this marvel of modern medicine is yours absolutely free with your purchase of any item on or about this wagon. Every item is reasonably priced; nothing over a dollar. Call out your desires."

A gruff man asked, "How much for them handcuffs?"

Mortimer looked at Amy and Joshua a little guiltily, then bent over and whispered to them, "*Psst.* I'll split the money with you, friends." Then he called down to the man, "Fifty cents for one pair; eighty-five cents for two. These bracelets have—ahem—held two of Dakota's most wanted individuals."

"Okay," said the man. "I'll take 'em." He handed Mortimer the money and Mortimer gave him both sets of handcuffs and a bottle of his all-season health tonic.

Mortimer sold some cups and a cookie cutter and two pairs of scissors. "Speak right up, friends. Anything at all on or about this wagon is yours for a silver dollar, or less. You may have the very shirt off my back."

Then a short man in front said, "I want your hat. How much?"

"I beg pardon? We have a large supply of headgear." Mortimer pointed to the hats on the shelf in the wagon. "Which, pray tell, do you fancy, sir?"

"The one on top of your head."

"Ah, what a pity. I'm afraid it's not for sale," said Mortimer.

"Oh yes it is," said the gruff man who had bought the handcuffs. "You said everything's for sale on or about the wagon, even the shirt off your back. If you don't sell that hat on your head to Jim Cothers here, I'll put these handcuffs on *you*. I'm a deputy sheriff in this here town. And you better not charge him more than a dollar neither."

"Ah yes," said Mortimer. "Deputy sheriff. Well, well. Sheriffs seem to abound in this town. Very law-abiding. Heartwarming thing . . ."

"Okay, now hand it over to Jim," warned the deputy sheriff, "or else!"

Joshua wondered if he should grab the hat and run. But just then Mortimer raised his hat cautiously above his head. The crowd gasped, then laughed, uproariously. For out of the magic hat another hat emerged and plopped down on Mortimer's head. Then a second and a third and a fourth and a fifth slid out, forming a stack of hats.

Mortimer said to Jim Cothers, "There you are, sir. A bit of legerdemain. For a mere fifty cents, you can have not *one* hat, but five, count them, five hats, each in topnotch condition, plus five bottles of all-season health tonic. The bargain of the century. And that, ladies, gents, boys, girls, dogs, and cats, concludes the sale for the day. Thank you kindly."

The crowd applauded as the man eagerly took the hats and medicine for the low price of fifty cents. Even the deputy sheriff was applauding, the handcuffs clanking in his hands. Then a woman's shrill voice was heard from the rear of the crowd. "Those two children. A dollar each. I want *them!*"

Amy and Joshua ducked down under the seat as Mortimer leaped to the reins. For the woman was Aunt Vootch! "Sheriff!" she screamed. "Make him sell those children! He swore he'd sell anything on the wagon."

"Sorry, lady," said the deputy sheriff. "He said the sale was over."

"Gee yap, Chrysanthemum. Gee yap, girl," called Mortimer softly. And in a flurry of rattles and jingles, Mortimer drove the wagon slowly, innocently away.

"He's a kidnaper!" shouted Aunt Vootch. "Arrest him!"

Then Amy had an idea. She stood up on the wagon seat so everyone could see and shouted back, "She's crazy! This man's my friend! He's taking us to our grandma and grandpa! She's just a loco second cousin!"

"Stop him, sheriff! *I* am their guardian!"

"Calm down, lady," said the deputy sheriff. "They don't look like they're being kidnaped none. Now you just tell me all about this. . . ."

The wagon moved out of earshot, rattling down the main street past the general store, the feed store and the railroad station. "Good work, Amy!" said Joshua. "You saved our skins."

"Ah well, well." Mortimer rubbed his nose. "It's half this way and half the other. I regret to say that now Madam Vootch knows our destination."

"Oh *no!*" Amy slapped her hand over her mouth. "I'm the dumbest bonehead in South Dakota!"

"Not at all. We are all subject to human error. If I'd started going east two days ago, we'd be in dear old Iowa by now. Well, well. Never fear. Once you're with your grand-papa, you'll be safe as a sardine in a salami factory. Now then, are we out of their view?"

"I think so," said Joshua. "Can't hardly see them anymore."

"Very good. All right, Chrysanthemum! Let's go!" He flicked the reins and the wagon raced ahead, east toward Iowa, at top speed.

8. THE IRON DRAGON

After half an hour Mortimer had to slow the pace, for Chrysanthemum was badly winded. Joshua kept watch at the rear of the wagon, but neither Aunt Vootch nor the deputy sheriff could be seen. He climbed back up front, and Amy asked Mortimer what he thought might have happened.

"I do believe your auntie Vootch went a shade too far. Trying to buy two children, as if they were a pair of bookends. Terrible. It does not gain the sympathy of crowd nor sheriff."

"Maybe she's given up," suggested Amy hopefully.

"Ah, that's doubtful. A woman with a whip hand like that never gives up. She's more likely going to try to reach New York before we do."

"How can she? We've got a horse and wagon," said Amy. "Won't we be able to get there pretty quick?"

"Oh, I should say in about two months if Chrysanthemum holds up and the wagon doesn't fall apart."

"Two months!" Joshua looked back toward the town. "That means she has two whole months to trap us. And she'll find a way. She always wins in the end. We'll *never* reach New York."

"Ah, worry, worry, worry. You are a worrier, young man. It gets us nowhere. We shall find us a speedier means of reaching the great city of New York City before you can say, 'A school of slippery sea serpents slowly slithered southward toward sunny San Francisco.' Don't try to repeat that; it will cause an injury to your tongue. By Samuel Quincy Morse! Do you see what I see along that hill?"

"Looks like telegraph poles," said Joshua.

"And what do you usually find running alongside a telegraph line?"

"Trains?" asked Amy.

"There you are! We've found our way east before you got to the word *slippery*. We'll follow the railroad tracks to the next town and board the train."

"But we don't have any tickets," said Joshua.

"And we can't get a ticket for Chrysanthemum," Amy added.

"Tush, tush, and a bucket of mush." Mortimer turned the wagon toward the telegraph line and tracks. "Keep your eyes open for a train. If one comes by, I'll dip into my hat. Perhaps a train will give it a gentle hint that three tickets are urgently desired. As for dear old Chrysanthemum, I fear she would never have made it past Iowa. Your aunt Vootch has been running poor old Chrysy ragged. We'll find some little farm for her to spend her final years in peace and plenty. She might pull a buggy to church on Sundays, nothing more. Fear not; I'll outwit your aunt Vootch or my name isn't Mortimer Q. Wintergreen."

"What's the Q stand for?" asked Amy.

"I shall never tell," answered Mortimer.

By then they were close enough to see the

tracks, which stretched all the way from the low hills in the west to the flat horizon in the east.

"Look! A train!" called Joshua. "Over there!"

"What! Where?" asked Mortimer.

"I see it, too," said Amy. "It's just a little puff of smoke."

"That's a cloud, I do believe. Wait! I have a telescope in the back. Got it with the parasols last month." Mortimer gave the reins to Joshua and climbed over the seat. He was back in a second with a little telescope.

Mortimer looked toward the west. "Aha. It is, indeed and indubitably, a locomotive. It should be passing by in a few minutes. Let's stop right here and wait. Whoa, Chrysanthemum!" Then he took his hat off and pointed it toward the oncoming train. "Just getting it in the right mood," he said.

As the train came closer, Mortimer passed the telescope to Amy. "Yowee!" she called. "It looks like it's coming straight at me!"

"Let me see!" said Joshua eagerly. "Come on, Amy, don't be such a big fat hog."

"Pass it back and forth, friends. But please

don't block the hat's view. Very sensitive chapeau, as I've sadly learned."

The train roared toward them, its thick black smoke billowing like a storm cloud. The green engine with its brass bell, and the yellow and red cars rattling behind, seemed like a puffing dragon raging forward to devour everyone and everything.

Then, with a great *whoosh*, the locomotive came thundering past, almost within reach. Mortimer had to calm Chrysanthemum, and Amy and Joshua were more than a little frightened themselves. But as the passenger cars rattled by, the iron dragon became a very human train, for there were men and women and children at the windows, and some of them were waving. Amy waved back, but as the last car passed by, her arm froze. For leaning out of a window, like the sting in a dragon's tail, was Aunt Vootch.

"It's her!" said Joshua, horrified. "I told you she'd follow us."

"Turn back!" called Aunt Vootch from the open window, as the train sped on. "Turn back, and I'll forgive and forget! Auntie Vootch always understands! Always! Always! Turn back, my darlings. . . ." Her voice faded as the train hurtled toward the east.

"Courage, children," said Mortimer. "Let's just hope our tickets will be for an express, so we can beat her to New York. Here we go! I'll try the hat."

Mortimer slipped his hand in, then looked into the hat, puzzled. "Strange. There's nothing here at all."

"Tickets can be pretty small," said Joshua. "Maybe they're hiding somewhere."

"Yes indeed. Here tickets, tickets, tickets. Come to Uncle Wintergreen. . . . Ah me. It's totally empty."

Then suddenly there was a tremendous *wuff* and a column of thick black smoke spurted from the hat.

"Acch . . . It's from the . . . acch, acch . . . from the train," Mortimer called, choking and coughing. He threw the hat as far as he could, but the smoke had already covered the entire wagon. Chrysanthemum was frightened half out of her wits; she dashed forward blindly while Mortimer tugged on the reins. "Whoa! Whoa—koff kaff ka-humpfh—whoa, girl!"

The frenzied dash helped clear the smoke away. Amy and Joshua tried to see what had happened, their eyes still burning from the smoke and soot. They saw the train at a standstill half a mile down the track; the engineer and fireman were climbing over the locomotive to check what was wrong. The big black stack stood high above the engine, but not a wisp of smoke emerged. And in the rear car, Aunt Vootch was leaning out of a window, pointing back toward their wagon with her whip.

When Mortimer brought Chrysanthemum under control, he turned the wagon back toward his hat, which was still discharging black sooty smoke. As they approached it, Chrysanthemum reared slightly and refused to budge. The hat was as frightening to Chrysanthemum as the locomotive had been. Mortimer climbed down from the wagon and edged toward his hat, circling it as the wind shifted, to avoid the billowing smoke. Then suddenly, there was a sound like water swirling down a drain, and the last of the smoke was sucked back into the hat.

At that same instant, black smoke shot up

from the locomotive's stack, and the drive rods started turning the wheels slowly, *ka-chaa, ka-chaa, ka-chaa, ka-chaa.* The engineer and fireman scrambled back up into the cab, and the train moved off toward the east.

"Ah me, ah me," said Mortimer, examining his hat gingerly. "Our lucky streak has ended. The hat's turned temperamental again. It needs a vacation." He rubbed a finger on the inside and a little puff of smoke came out. "Not done yet, eh? My, my."

"Mr. Mortimer," asked Amy, "don't you think we could sort of just sneak onto a train without tickets?"

"No, no! Railroad conductors can be as ferocious as sheriffs. We'll simply hold a sale in the next town. Everything on the wagon must go, including the wagon. We'll buy our tickets with the money we make. Don't fret, I'll get you safely to New York, by hook or crooked dice."

9. THE IDEA OF THE CENTURY

They rode along, following the railroad tracks, and within an hour they saw a large town in the distance.

"Ah," said Mortimer. "That must be the town of Mitchell. Excellent spot for a wagon sale. Happy memories of past visits. Yes indeed. Very pleasant jail, highest recommendation."

"Look at those colored things in the sky." Amy pointed toward the south side of town. "They look like big upside-down pears."

"By Joseph Q. Montgolfier, those aren't pears. Those are aerial balloons." Mortimer clapped his telescope to his eye. "Three of them, as pretty as you please. They must be having a fair. Excellent! We'll sell out the wagon in no time."

"Do you mean those are the kind of balloons people can go up in?" asked Joshua. Neither he nor Amy had ever seen a passenger balloon, though they had read about them in school.

"The very same. Just like climbing a tall tree, but twenty times as high. Greatest thrill in the world, next to eating a good sirloin steak, medium rare."

After buying eggs and milk and other supplies, Mortimer drove the wagon directly to the fairgrounds. They were soon riding down the midway past games of chance, shooting galleries, sideshows, and a carousel. As the wagon rumbled along, Amy nudged Mortimer. "Look, Mr. Mortimer. That man selling candy apples. He's waving to you."

"And he's only got one arm," said Joshua.

Mortimer raised his hat in greeting as they drove by. "I do believe I've seen that gentleman before, somewhere. My, my . . ."

"Golly," Amy whispered to Joshua. "He must be the man who pulled the lion out of the hat."

"Tiger," corrected Mortimer, as he tipped his hat once more.

Toward the far end of the midway, Mortimer noticed an empty spot. He brought the wagon around and backed it into position.

"Perfect. Our grand sale will take place right here. Children, here's twenty-five cents for each of you. Wander about. Purchase a spicy sausage or three. I can handle everything myself. Come back in a couple of hours and we'll be ready to buy our train tickets."

"Oh thanks, Mr. Mortimer!" called Amy, jumping off the wagon. "Thanks, thanks, thanks!"

"Mention it not," said Mortimer. "It is a joy to see you joyful. Besides, I'll add it to my bill when we reach your dear old grandpa."

"What if we spot Aunt Vootch?" asked Joshua.

"Aha. You're a born pessimist, young man. Bad. I shall have to give you lessons in optimism and general upness. Look at me. Not a care in the world, except for an honest desire to be a millionaire. However, if you should see your aunt, my advice is simple and to the point. *Run!*"

Amy and Joshua sped down the midway toward the three giant balloons. Each balloon was held to the ground by a tether, a long rope to keep it from floating away, and each was beautifully decorated with yellow and blue fringes. The words *Calcott's Carnival Balloons, the Best in South Dakota* were written in great blue letters on the side of each gas bag.

Beneath the balloons were the passenger gondolas, huge square baskets that could each hold six people. As one balloon went up with its passengers, a second slowly descended. And a third was held fast to the ground by guy ropes, while six new passengers came aboard. There was a line of thirty or forty people waiting to go up. A sign read:

RIDE A CALCOTT CARNIVAL BALLOON,

SEE AS FAR AS NEBRASKA.

ADULTS, HALF DOLLAR.

CHILDREN, A QUARTER.

NO SMOKING OR SLINGSHOTS PERMITTED.

"A quarter!" said Joshua. "That's all we've got for everything. How bad do you want to go up, Amy?"

Joshua didn't want to go up at all; the very thought made him dizzy. The balloon on the ground was as large as a house, but the one overhead was so high, it seemed smaller than the quarter in his hand. He hoped Amy would say no.

"Well . . ." said Amy. "I'd rather go on the carousel and eat watermelon. And sausages."

"Okay, I agree," said Joshua. "But why don't you admit *you're* scared this time!"

"I'm not scared! At all!" Just then Amy noticed a little sign off to one side:

CHILDREN MUST BE
ACCOMPANIED BY ADULTS.

"Look at that," she said. "We can't go up anyway."

"Well, I'm an adult," said Joshua.

"If you are, why do you always carry those stupid guns around, with no bullets in them!"

"Don't worry!" said Joshua. "I'll get the bullets."

In the next hour, Amy and Joshua explored the fair from one end to the other and back. As they debated a third ride on the carousel, Joshua thought it might be right and proper to return some of the money to Mortimer and not spend it all. So with ten cents remaining between them, they went back to the wagon.

Mortimer sat gloomily on the seat, munching peanuts. "Ah me," he said, as Amy and Joshua climbed up beside him. "Business has been worse than dismal. In the entire time you've been gone, I sold one, count it, one comb. For two cents. It seems that folks at a fair aren't interested in used knicker-knacks. But there's no use crying over spilled sarsaparilla. I'll just have to think of something else."

Amy held out her hand. "We've got ten cents back for you. Does that help any?"

"Well, we could buy three more bags of peanuts in a pinch," said Mortimer. "Have some."

"We almost went up in one of them balloons," said Joshua, taking a handful of peanuts. "But it cost a quarter each. And there was a line as long as a church aisle."

"A line, eh?" Mortimer rubbed his chin in thought. "Yes indeed. Those balloons are the biggest attraction in the fair. My brain is beginning to nip at the edge of an invention. Why not? It could work! It might! It might! Get ready, friends. Mortimer Q. Wintergreen has just gotten the idea of the century!" Then he took the reins and drove the wagon down the midway, toward the balloons.

At the balloon ride, Mortimer climbed down from the wagon to talk to the ticket seller. The man looked at Mortimer as if he were insane, then turned and stared at Chrysanthemum and the wagon and burst out laughing. He called another man over, who shook his head in disbelief while Mortimer spoke. But as Mortimer continued, gesturing toward the wagon, the two men started to scratch their heads and debate with each other.

"What's going on?" Joshua asked Amy, who was making a quick sketch of the balloons. "Think he's selling everything?"

"I don't know," said Amy. "I'd sneak over and listen, except it wouldn't be exactly polite. Besides, they'd see me. Too bad there are no bushes."

Then suddenly, both men shook hands with Mortimer. He returned to the wagon, whistling a waltz tune.

"Well, well, my small companions. We're going to have a sale after all. We'll have our train tickets by the end of the day."

"But how?" asked Amy.

"Wait and see. We have to be back here in an hour. That's when our wagon turns into a golden pumpkin. In the meantime, I wish to have a ride on the carousel. Haven't been on one since I was a young sprout."

Mortimer and the children went on the carousel twice, then crossed the midway to watch a pie-eating contest. "Makes your mouth want to cry," said Mortimer. "The only contest that's as much fun to lose as to win."

They wandered about awhile longer, then returned to their wagon. Amy and Joshua were surprised to see all three balloons down, and an enormous crowd gathered around them. A new sign had been freshly painted:

FIRST TIME IN HISTORY!
THE ASCENT BY BALLOON
OF A HORSE AND WAGON!
SEE IT HERE! SEE IT NOW!

"Look!" Amy said. "They must mean Chrysanthemum!"

"Ah yes, indeed. Chrysy and I are about to venture upward. However, you and Joshua may stay behind if you wish."

Mortimer drove the wagon under the balloons, which were hovering just a little above the ground. The three baskets beneath had been removed, but the support ropes still hung down from the huge gas bags.

"I want to go up, too," called Amy quickly.

"Splendid," said Mortimer. Then he and Amy turned and looked at Joshua.

"I—uh," he stammered. "I don't—I don't think I want to go, just now. . . ."

"Very good," said Mortimer. "I'll arrange for you to wait with the ticket seller. Now what we're going to do is as easy as pie à la mode. They're going to attach all three balloons to Chrysanthemum and the wagon. And then we'll hold our sale. Every item we sell will make the wagon that much lighter. And at some point our weight will just equal the upward pull of the balloons. Then one more item sold—it could be as small as a thimble—and up we go. We keep half the money from the sale and the balloon operators get the other half. Simple, is it not?"

As Mortimer spoke, the men busily tied the balloons' support lines to the wagon, while their assistants slipped a leather harness under and around Chrysanthemum, and tied more supports to the harness.

Joshua stood up, ashamed of his fear, yet eager to get off the wagon. Mortimer and Amy had climbed to the rear to prepare for the sale.

How could Amy not be scared, Joshua wondered. It was impossible! She was acting so calm just to show off and get him mad.

Joshua suddenly plopped back down on the seat. "Okay! I'm going, too!" he announced. "And that's that!"

"Good, brave lad," said Mortimer as he bustled among the bottles and parasols. Then he lowered the canvas sides and called to the crowd. "Every item is for sale except my horse, my hat, and these two brave children. *And* my friends, as an added bonus, a prize of five—count them—five silver dollars will be awarded to the individual who purchases the final item which, when removed from this wagon, lightens it just enough to permit us to venture skyward. It may be a child's top or a bottle of all-season health tonic. Very well. Who will buy the first item?"

As word spread through the fair, the crowd around the wagon grew to a huge mob. Amy and Joshua had to help Mortimer keep track of the frantic bidding. It seemed as if everyone in the town of Mitchell wanted to win the five silver dollars and see the horse and wagon rise into the sky.

But after an hour of hectic selling, the wagon was still earthbound, though almost all the merchandise was gone. "Ah me," said Mortimer. "Maybe we're being weighted down with all this money. In order to ascend, we may have to throw away some of our silver dollars. Very uncivilized. My fingers tremble at the thought."

Someone bought the six-shooters that had belonged to the bandits. Joshua hesitated, looked toward Amy, and then asked Mortimer whether he thought they ought to sell their own silver-plated guns, to lighten the wagon further. It pained Joshua to ask; those guns—no matter what Amy thought—made him feel stronger, bigger, taller than he was. Still, it was only right to offer.

"Never," said Mortimer. "I'd sooner sell my hat from off my head."

Joshua sighed with relief, though he felt guilty at the same time. Well, Mr. Mortimer wasn't selling his hat! Wasn't that hat Mr. Mortimer's gun, in a way?

A little girl called out from the crowd, "I'll give you a dime for that book." She pointed at Amy's sketchbook, lying on the front seat of the wagon.

"*Psst,*" Mortimer whispered to Amy. "I'll tell her it's yours and not for sale."

"Wait!" said Amy. "I'll sell her *half* the book. Okay? The front half. She can have the drawings I've made. I'd rather keep the blank pages because that's the drawings I haven't made yet." Amy tore the book along the binding and in a moment there were two thinner books in her hand.

"Ah yes," said Mortimer. "Half a book for only half a dime! A mere nickel!"

Amy tossed the front half of the book to

the little girl. And softly, silkily, like syrup flowing from an open jug, the wagon rose from the ground: one foot, two feet, three . . .

As the crowd roared, Chrysanthemum whinnied and started to gallop, but there was no longer any earth to gallop upon. Her hooves churned against empty air. Mortimer leaned out from the wagon and tossed the prize of five silver dollars to the little girl, then turned to calm Chrysanthemum.

They rose with the balloons as the men below let out more and more of the tether rope. Twenty feet, thirty, forty . . . They could see the tops of the tents below them, and then they were higher than the highest trees.

"Ah, what a glorious view!" said Mortimer. "Something to tell your grandchildren. We are rising into the sky like a kite on that tether rope. Will wonders never cease!"

Joshua couldn't believe it; he wasn't afraid anymore. Mortimer's calmness had calmed him, too. As a bird flew past the wagon, Joshua recalled a dream he had once had in

which he'd been flying, flying away from Aunt
Vootch and the bullies at school. The dream
had been sweet, but this reality was even
better. It made him feel brave, somehow,
like a knight in a high tower.

As they ascended, Amy stared over the
side of the wagon. At three hundred feet,
the people below seemed like mechanical
dolls on top of an elaborate music box. "It
looks as if you could just pick everybody up
and put them all in your pocket," she said.

Mortimer tipped his hat to the cheering
crowd, then took the reins and called, "Gee
yap, Chrysanthemum! Wait! Wait a minute. Slight error. We aren't going anywhere.
How embarrassing. Whoa, Chrysanthemum!
Whoa!"

Suddenly, a strong gust of wind blew Mortimer's hat off. It flew to the back of the
wagon and landed upside down, near the
water bucket. Joshua climbed over the seat
and lunged for it just as another gust lifted
it toward the edge of the wagon. Joshua caught
it by the brim in midflight, just in time.

"Well done," said Mortimer. "You've saved

my chapeau from flying to the moon."

Joshua felt a surge of power; for these few seconds the hat was his. What if he put his hand inside and tried his luck? He was sure the hat liked him, too. Maybe, instead of crayons, it would give him bullets for his gun.

He let himself daydream for a moment, as the wagon swung beneath the balloons. If he could control the hat, he could be a real magician, just like Mr. Mortimer. Maybe he could become his assistant. Or even get a hat of his own someday. Wouldn't *that* be something! No one would dare push him around ever again. Well, he would try his luck! Right now!

He held the hat over one of the guns stuck in his belt, to hint gently that he wanted bullets. Then he eased his left hand into the hat, keeping his back to Mortimer so he couldn't see. The hat seemed empty. . . .

Suddenly, at the bottom, he felt the rough grizzled end of a rope. Joshua gave one great pull and out came the rope, yard after yard. It wasn't bullets, but it was as good as Mortimer's trick in his magic show.

"Look!" Joshua shouted. "I can get things from the hat, too!"

"Ah no!" shouted Mortimer. "You shouldn't have done that! No! It could have been a ferocious thing. A man-eating eagle, or worse."

"It's just another clothesline," said Amy, as more and more rope came out of the hat.

"Thunderation!" called Mortimer. "It *is* ferocious! That's no clothesline! It's the tether for the balloons! The rope they used to hold us to the ground! The hat's doing it again! No end of trouble! We're rising into the clouds! We're floating free! How very, very embarrassing."

10. A GIGGLE OF GEESE

As the balloons rose higher and higher, the fairgrounds below became another patch of color in the crazy quilt of green and yellow fields stretching to the horizon. The earth seemed so far away that, Amy thought, if she fell she might float forever. She wished she could draw it all, but she knew she could never capture the vastness of it.

The wind grew stronger as they rose, making the support lines hum and vibrate. A sudden angry gust forced the balloons to bump against one another, while Chrysanthemum and the wagon swung helplessly beneath. Joshua felt a surge of fear again, as the wagon dipped and swayed.

Mortimer grabbed the tether and quickly

tied Joshua and Amy to the wagon seat, then fastened his hat to his head with a pair of suspenders. "Sit tight, friends!" he shouted. "All is well! A trifling breeze."

Joshua sat glumly silent, angry at his own stupidity. What could he say to them? They were probably about to plummet to their deaths. And he, Joshua, had done it, by fooling with the hat at the worst possible time. Mortimer was right: The hat *was* temperamental. And dangerous!

As they pressed themselves hard against the wagon seat, great patches of mist swept past them, covering their hands and faces with a wet film.

"Fear not," said Mortimer. "We're entering a cloud."

In a moment they were surrounded by a thick grayish-white fog. They could scarcely see Chrysanthemum's ears up ahead. But the balloons still bumped and curtsied with every change of wind, and the wagon still swayed dizzily.

"I'm getting seasick," said Mortimer. "But stout hearts and strong stomachs! Remember, so long as we're in a cloud, we're safe.

Clouds do not crash into barns or chicken coops. Let us whistle a few cheery tunes to keep up our spirits, as sailors do on sinking ships. Do you children know 'Yo-Ho, Blow the Man Down!'?"

Although Joshua could scarcely hear him over the wind, Mortimer's whistling made him feel as if they were heroes laughing at danger. Even Chrysanthemum seemed calmer. Maybe we won't crash after all, he thought. Maybe he's still got something up his sleeve. Or his hat.

The mist continued, hour after hour. If there was any world left, they couldn't tell; their universe ended at the edge of the wagon and the tops of the balloons. Above, below, around them, the gray mist churned and re-shaped like a horde of troubled ghosts.

Joshua's ears were aching from the height, and he and Amy were shivering from the cold and wetness.

"Ah well," said Mortimer, "there's more than one way to cook an onion. What you need is a triple dose of Wintergreen's All-Season Health Tonic; good for shivers and sweats, among one hundred and seventeen other common ailments of humankind." He felt around in his jacket pocket and pulled out two small bottles. "There you are. Shake well before using."

Amy and Joshua made wry faces as they raised the bottles to their mouths. But the tonic was as sweet as honey and almost as thick. "This isn't like Aunt Vootch's rotten tonic at all," said Amy.

"A few swallows of this would cure Madam Vootch of many an ill. Finish up, my small companions. Down the hatch."

They drank the rest of the tonic, though it was hard to hold the bottles steady as the wagon dipped and swayed. "My stomach feels sort of funny," said Joshua.

"Nothing to fear. One of my priceless in-gredients is undoubtedly reacting with an-other priceless ingredient."

"My hands feel hot," said Amy.

"And my feet!" shouted Joshua over a gust of wind.

"Yes indeed. My health tonic is not for the weak of heart nor lame of courage. When the wagon starts to spin in rapid circles, think nothing of it. It's merely the tonic telling you how happy it is to be a guest in your stomachs. Just close your eyes and smile."

In a few moments, Amy and Joshua were warm from top to toe, and the wagon did seem to be going round and round, like a carousel at the fair, but very gently. If the balloons were bumping, they no longer felt it. The last thing Amy remembered before she fell asleep was someone pushing a jacket between her head and the wagon seat. Some-one who said over and over, "Sleep like the dickens! Sleep like the dickens!"

It seemed to Amy that only a few minutes had passed before she awoke. Her arms and legs were stiff from the crouched position she'd taken against the seat. She opened her eyes, squinting in the sun's dazzle.

The sky was a clean, clear blue. Above her head, the three huge pear-shaped gas bags were floating in quiet majesty. A mile below, the earth was an endless mantle of rippling gray-green, speckled here and there with little black lakes that suddenly flashed in the sun. And behind her, in the wagon,

Joshua was helping Mortimer fry some of the eggs he'd bought on the way to the fair-grounds.

Amy watched in amazement; there was no fire, yet the eggs were sizzling in the flapjack pan. Mortimer had fashioned a reflector from an old tin box, and the flapjack pan had grown scorching hot in the doubly intense sunlight.

"The sun's a glorious thing," said Mortimer. "We'll have to do our cooking early or late, when the shadows of the balloons don't cover us."

While Amy and Joshua ate their eggs with big slabs of bread, Mortimer attached a pail of oats to a long pole, leaned forward at the front of the wagon, and fed Chrysanthemum.

"Good girl," he said. "Finest floating horse in North America. By Daniel Q. Webster, we're doing quite comfortably up here, now that the wind has turned steady. Speaking of wind, which way is it to the east, again, young man?"

Joshua pointed straight ahead.

"And that's just where this wind is propelling us. We are being flung toward the east at a heartwarmingly rapid rate. My hat may not be as dumb as it looks. Perhaps it flew off my head yesterday to tempt you, young man, so that you could pull the tether loose, so that we could rise up into the higher reaches of the atmosphere, so that we could be bobbled about by the winds, so that we could be blown eastward toward the city of New York City, so that we could reach your grandma and grandpa, so that I could receive a handsome reward as well as appear on the stage as the greatest magician in the northern hemisphere. That's the kind of hat this hat can be, when it wants to be that kind of hat."

Maybe Mortimer was right, thought Joshua. Maybe the hat had been trying to help. Well, in that case, he might just try once more to get some bullets—but only when they were safely on the ground again.

"Have we reached Iowa yet, Mr. Mortimer?" Amy asked as she watched the farms below slide past in great squares of yellow and green.

"Excellent question. Unfortunately, I no longer possess my telescope. Sold it yesterday for seventy cents. But I would say we're over either Wisconsin or Madagascar. They're both this color from the sky, I do believe."

"Look! Over there!" said Joshua. "Up ahead. It's all bluish gray."

Off in the distance, at the edge of the horizon, the yellow and green stopped abruptly, and a vast crescent of blue began.

"It's Lake Erie!" called Amy. "Or maybe Lake Superior."

Mortimer shielded his eyes with his hand, and looked off into the distance. "Ah me, no. It's Lake Wisconsin, to be sure."

"But there's no such thing," said Joshua.

"Correcting your elders again, eh? Soon you'll want to be captain of this entire wagon. Have I reached so sorry a state that children scarcely large enough to sneeze can tell Mortimer Q. Wintergreen which side is down? Never! If I say that's Lake Wisconsin below, then it's Lake Wisconsin. Even if it's actually Lake Michigan, which is what I meant in the first place. Now then—"

Amy suddenly interrupted. "Below! Look below!"

There, far beneath the wagon, was a flight

of geese spread out in a wide V formation. Joshua thought he could hear them honking as they flew.

"Let's feed them!" Amy took chunks of bread left over from breakfast and threw them down toward the geese.

"They'll never get it," said Joshua. "The wind's blowing it to the side. See. You've missed by a mile. Let *me* try."

Joshua squeezed some bread into pellets and threw them as far out from the wagon as he could. "He got it! Come on! Let's send some more down."

Amy and Joshua made more bread pellets, and Mortimer took some oats from Chrysanthemum's pail. In a moment, a barrage of oats and bread sprayed down from the wagon, and the geese started climbing to meet the shower of food. Up they came, still in V formation, rising toward the floating horse and wagon.

"We need more bread!" called Joshua. "Get the loaf, Amy. Hurry!"

There wasn't time to press the bread into pellets, for the geese were next to the wagon by now. Amy and Joshua tore bits of bread from the loaf and hurled them out at the hungry, honking geese.

Then one of the geese settled on the wagon, nipping at bread crumbs and oats on the wagon floor. A second alighted, and a third. Two more geese perched on Chrysanthemum's back, and three on top of the gas bags. Then all the others flew down, and the wagon resounded with the calls of honking geese and the voice of Mortimer Wintergreen.

"Oh sauerkraut!" he called. "We've been invaded! There's no room to think. It's a whole giggle of geese. Shoo! Shoo, geese! Fly! Flee!" But the geese simply scurried and fluttered out of reach, then settled down to search for more bread crumbs. "Ah me. They're getting a free ride and they know it. A smart goose's goose is never cooked."

"Look!" called Joshua, pointing from the side of the wagon. "It's all blue below. Whichever lake it is, we're over it."

Amy watched from the other side. "We're going down. I can see little ripples and waves."

"Sauerkraut! Sauerkraut!" Mortimer bellowed. "The geese are weighing us down.

We're about to sink into the drink! Shoo! Shoo!"

Mortimer, Amy, and Joshua waved their arms and jumped and shouted. But the geese flew up, with a flurry of wings, and perched on top of the balloons.

Mortimer jumped toward the box of dishes. "We've got to lighten up! Here goes the flap-jack pan!"

They watched the pan tumble downward and hit the water with a little white splash. Then Mortimer threw the tin box over, followed by two parasols left from the sale. One of them opened on the way down, floated gracefully for a moment, then hit the water.

"No use! We're still sinking!"

Mortimer threw some knives and forks over the side, followed by a bag of apples, half the oats, and a dozen eggs. The wagon was only a few hundred feet above the water now, and still descending rapidly.

"This calls for drastic action. Help me, Joshua." Mortimer cut the canvas cover loose from the wagon and shoved it over, into the water. Then he took hold of a side board and yanked it loose with Joshua's help. And another board, and another.

As Chrysanthemum's front legs skimmed along the surface of the water, Mortimer tore the tailgate off the wagon. He swung it at the geese, shouting, "Shoo! SHOOO!" But again they flew out of reach. Mortimer threw the tailgate into the water and rushed forward to tear out the front seat.

"We're going up!" called Amy. "Chrysanthemum's out of the water! We're rising!"

"A sight for sore ears. The best part of my wagon's floating in Lake Minnesota, but at least we haven't drowned. Don't go near the sides of the wagon, friends. Because there are no sides left."

11. HELLO, C. P.!

The wagon was still rising too sluggishly, so Mortimer poured some of their drinking water overboard to help bring them quickly to a safe height. Then, satisfied that all was well, he lay down in the back for a long afternoon nap. As he turned sideways, he clutched his hat to his chest with both arms.

"He doesn't trust me anymore," Joshua whispered to Amy.

"Why should he? You might pull Lake Michigan out of his hat and drown us all."

"But Mr. Mortimer said that maybe it was a good thing, what happened. So maybe the hat actually likes me, same as you."

"I don't think you should touch it any-more, Joshua!"

"Don't worry, I won't."

Wisps of clouds appeared, like flecks of foam on a bright, calm sea. As the geese settled down to preen their feathers and di-gest their lunch, Amy and Joshua began counting the clouds. It proved to be a hectic game. There would suddenly be a group above them, then below, then to the side. The clouds seemed to come out of nowhere. And every so often they went right through one, scarcely larger than the wagon itself. But soon the clouds dispersed, and they saw they were over land again.

Toward evening, as they and the geese nibbled on cheese and bread from their sup-plies, they watched the setting sun transform the western sky into a procession of long red banners stretching to the horizon. Amy took the remaining half of her sketchbook and drew the sunset quickly, using her new red and orange crayons.

"A majestic moment," said Mortimer. "Sunset from a mile up. Gaze upon it, children. Draw it while the drawing's good, young lady. Even Chrysanthemum knows a first-rate sirloin sunset when she sees one."

That night they took turns standing watch to make sure that all was well with the balloons and the wagon and Chrysanthemum. The wind remained steady and the stars opened one by one, like white wildflowers. And below, on the tar-black earth, an occasional cluster of flickering lights marked the towns and villages.

Amy looked longingly at one small cluster, wishing she could be down there, in that town, in a bed in a house with a mother and father, and warm smells of food, and the yellow of a kerosene lantern, the way it had been long ago, before Larison's Creek. She watched the twinkling lights grow dimmer and dimmer as the town slid behind her into the darkness. If only she could draw that black, black emptiness and make it seem safe and friendly, somehow, like a tame black bear. Instead of this feeling of loneliness. If only she could.

During his watch, Joshua spotted an orange-red glow in the distance. He wondered whether it was a forest fire, or an iron foundry, or, possibly, an undiscovered volcano. Or the firebox of Aunt Vootch's locomotive, racing eastward. The thought made him shudder. Well, soon, soon, they would be safe from her, once and for all. Soon Aunt Vootch would just be a bad memory.

The next morning they had bread and cheese for breakfast. Mortimer was tempted to try the hat for muffins or a bit of jam, but decided it would be dangerous to test its mood again, while hanging in the clouds.

The geese clustered around for their share of the bread, and soon the loaf was gone. "Well, well," said Mortimer, "we may have to start eating Chrysanthemum's oats. Our cupboard is almost bare. If you're still hungry, you may chew on your fingernails. They need clipping anyway."

The wind blew steadily all morning, rocking the wagon gently as the balloons carried them farther and farther eastward. Every so often, Mortimer stood up, hand to his forehead, and scanned the distant horizon.

"Nothing but low mountains, far as the eye can spy."

"Probably the Alleghenies," suggested Joshua.

"The Adirondacks," said Amy.

"Neither, friends. Those are the famous Nimwontapon Mountains of Pennsylvania, to be sure, to be sure."

"Never heard of them," said Joshua.

"There is always a first time to gain wisdom, young man. *Nim* means tall, *won* means long, *ta* means short, and *pon* means orange, in Indian talk. Those are, consequently, the tall, long, short, orange mountains. Wait, wait. They're not orange. Great Caesar's scissors! They must be the Appalachians! We're almost there! We're approaching the great state of New Jersey. All hands on deck! It's time to descend!"

As if sensing the end of the journey, the largest of the geese flapped its wings and rose from the wagon. And instantly, the other geese honked loudly and rose in a black, brown, and white swirl of wings and feathers.

"No!" shouted Mortimer. "Come back! We

need weight now. Oh sauerkraut, sauerkraut! Come back!" But the geese re-formed their V, and turned toward the north.

With the geese gone from the wagon, the lightened balloons shuddered then rose straight up like three puffs of smoke.

"By Benjamin Quincy Harrison's beard! We need weight! Weight! I fear we're heading for Mars or Jupiter or points beyond!"

"Maybe you could pull some horseshoes from your hat," suggested Joshua.

"We'll have to try it," said Mortimer. "But if my hat gives us the ropes tying our wagon to the balloons up there, remember as you plunge to earth to say a rapid prayer."

Mortimer hesitated a moment, then reached into his hat and took out a black crayon. "Well, well. Another small gift for you, young lady. Unfortunately, it doesn't weigh enough. We must press on!"

He quickly drew from the hat a broken bottle, a bunch of scallions, an eagle's nest, and a shoe, followed by a crowbar, a hammer, and a broken bugle. "Ah! Our hat's getting the message! This is the weight we need!"

As the giant gas bags slowed their rise, hovered, then started to gently descend, Amy studied the black crayon. She squeezed the crayon tightly as she recalled her empty feeling in the darkness, and her wish that she could have drawn it. Could the hat have guessed what she'd been feeling then, she wondered.

The balloons continued their descent over the low mountains of western New Jersey and across the rolling hills. As towns and farms passed by beneath them, they noticed, in the distant haze, streaks and squares of reflected sunlight, as if the earth were holding up a thousand mirrors.

"That's it!" said Mortimer. "Children! Children! Prepare for the sight of a lifetime!"

The haze lifted all at once, and the Hudson River was suddenly before them. And beyond, they saw the gleaming skyline of Manhattan. Amy and Joshua stared until they felt dizzy. They had been awed by pictures of New York, but the cluster of high buildings at the southern tip of Manhattan, and the miles and miles of smaller buildings, seemed to cover the entire earth.

"Glorious! Glorious!" called Mortimer. "The city of New York City, complete with shops, ships, and charlatans. There's the Tower Building, that tall one over there. Can you see? And there to the south! The Brooklyn Bridge! It's grand! I'm back, city of New York City! Mortimer Q. Wintergreen is back! Look! To the east! Central Park! Hello, C. P.! I'm back! Your far-wandering friend has returned. We've arrived, everybody. We've arrived. Let's descend fast, before we end up in the Atlantic Ocean. Come on, hat! I need more weight! Give me some cannon balls! Anchors! Elephants! It's time for work!"

12. SLICKENS

Mortimer reached into the hat again and again, and with scarcely a glance, tossed everything into the back of the wagon: a potato, a bag of pencil shavings, a dictionary, a brick, two spoons, and a beer mug with the words *God Save the Queen* on the side. The balloons were only a few hundred feet off the ground and rapidly approaching the level of the rooftops. "By Christopher Q. Columbus, I've got to steer!" called Mortimer. "We may land in someone's fireplace, like good old Saint Nick."

They were approaching a church steeple; the spire lay dead ahead. Mortimer tugged on the reins and Chrysanthemum twisted and turned, as best she could, causing the balloons to tilt. The wagon swung clear as they passed, but a rear wheel nicked the steeple and started spinning.

As they passed over Central Park West, several carriages bounced up onto the sidewalk as their frightened drivers tried to avoid the traffic coming at them out of the sky. The balloons were only some fifty feet above the ground now, and coming down fast.

"Lighten up! Lighten up!" Mortimer shouted to Joshua. "We're going to hit too hard!"

Joshua threw the bugle and crowbar over the side of the wagon, and the descent slowed.

As they floated over the heads of the amazed strollers in Central Park, Mortimer shouted to them, "Make way! Make way for Mortimer Q. Wintergreen, the greatest magician in the entire solar system! Come one, come all, to the magic show! Time to be announced! Theater to be announced! Remember the name! Wintergreen!"

They were approaching a wide meadow on which dozens of couples were playing lawn tennis. The white balls crisscrossed back and forth like tiny meteors.

"We'll have to land there," Mortimer called. "Here we go!"

People leaped to left and right as the horse and wagon came hurtling toward them. The wheels were ten feet off the ground, five feet. Chrysanthemum's legs tore down the tennis nets arranged one after another along the length of the field. Then the wheels touched the ground and Chrysanthemum's hooves were dragged through the grass, for the balloons were still pulling the wagon forward faster than the horse could gallop. And every so often the balloons surged upward, raising the wagon off the ground again and setting it down with a jolt.

"Pull the rip panels!" a man in the crowd shouted up to them. "The rip panels! Let out the gas!"

But Mortimer was frantically cutting all the connecting ropes around the wagon. Then he leaped onto Chrysanthemum's back and cut all the lines holding her harness to the balloons. One by one the freed balloons shot skyward and floated single file toward the east.

An angry crowd of tennis players gathered

round the horse and wagon, waving their rackets threateningly.

"This isn't a carriageway!" a man with a handlebar mustache shouted.

"Our nets are twisted together like spaghetti!" called a woman.

"Indecent behavior on a Sunday afternoon!"

"Madman!"

"Lunatic!"

"Fool!"

Mortimer stood on the wagon seat and raised his hands for silence. "My gentle followers of the goodly game of tennis! May I have your kindliest attention. I offer you massive apologies for your tangled nets and trampled turf. The wind played tricks on us and my horse lost her way. If you wish to sue, please contact my attorneys, Larabee, Harabee, and Smollens, at Seventeen North Main Street, Deadwood, South Dakota, U.S.A. But remember, my friends, once and once only in your lifetime will you have seen the sight you saw: a horse and wagon dropping from the clouds to herald the arrival of Wintergreen's Magnificent Marathon Magic Show. Theater to be announced; time to be announced. And because you have been so kind, you are all invited to attend for half price. Simply repeat the phrase 'a mess of tennis nets' at the box office and you'll receive two tickets for the price of one. I thank you for your kind solicitude."

The crowd seemed satisfied, ruined tennis nets notwithstanding.

"What an announcement!" someone said.

"Great showmanship!"

"P. T. Barnum couldn't have done better!"

"Splendid entertainment!"

"Enterprising!"

Mortimer tipped his hat, called "Gee yap" to Chrysanthemum, and drove toward the nearest carriage road, uprooting another row of tennis nets along the way. Once on the road, he headed toward the east side of the park. "We're on our way to your grand old grandfolks, friends. I'm sure a hearty repast will be forced upon us, not to mention rewards beyond a poor magician's wildest dreams. What was that address again, young man?"

Joshua searched in his pockets and found

their letter. "It says here: 328 Fifth Avenue, New York."

"So it is. A gilt-edged address. They live elbow to elbow with millionaires, business tycoons, swindlers, and other people of eminence and importance. We'll take Fifth Avenue all the way down, and you'll be able to see the mansions of the upper cruller."

As they rode down Fifth Avenue, Amy and Joshua turned from left to right and back. They couldn't believe so many magnificent buildings could be crowded one after another on a single avenue. Who had had the time to build them all?

Mortimer pointed out one vast structure after another. "And there's the home of Cornelius Q. Vanderbilt, a name that bounces like silver dollars within my brain."

Amy realized that Mortimer must have been right all along. Her grandparents were obviously rich. They *had* to be rich to live along this avenue. She would have a hundred beautiful dresses to replace her faded blue cotton one. And she'd have lemonade and chocolate cake whenever she liked, and dolls made of china and silk, and rings to wear, and white shoes. But best of all, she would have her own snug bedroom at last, safe from the darkness, with the voices of her grandparents just beyond the door.

"Over there's the mansion of John Jacob Astor. And your grandparents are right on the next block! Friends, you've been born with a gold spoon in your noodle soup!"

"Ya-hoo!" shouted Joshua. "We should've run away a million years ago."

In another minute they were at the front door of 328 Fifth Avenue. The mansion was almost as tall and stately as the Astor building. Mortimer adjusted his necktie and collar, combed Joshua's hair with his pocket comb, then took the big black door knocker shaped like a lion's head and gave three solid, dignified raps. "Now remember, we are amongst the upper crumb cake. No fidgeting. No ear scratching. And do not speak until you have been poked by me."

The door opened, and a man wearing a dark suit and stiff white shirt appeared. He stood erect with his chin high. "Yes? May I ask the nature of your business?"

"The name is Wintergreen. Mortimer Q.

These children are none other than your own kith and kin from the wilds of South Dakota. Amy and Joshua, meet your grandpater."

"I beg your pardon," said the man. "I am Slickens, the butler. Did you perchance say Amy and Joshua?"

"And Mortimer Q. Now then, Slickens, would you be so good as to call Mr. Baines. You may tell him that we have arrived. Here, sir, is my calling card." He held out a small card to Slickens.

"So sorry. Mr. and Mrs. Baines are no longer with us."

Mortimer dropped the calling card. "But— but that's impossible. They own this very house!"

"Ah," said Slickens. "If you'd be so good as to come round to the kitchen door, I be-lieve I can ease your mind on that most in-teresting matter. Round that hedge, to your left."

They went to the back door and Slickens showed them into the kitchen. "Miss Cog-glesworth," he said to the maid, "would you give these children some crackers and milk and the gentleman a spot of the caviar and port wine we've been having for our, ahem, lunch. . . . Now then, I regret to tell you that the Baineses do not own this house. I daresay they don't own anything. She was merely the cook here and he was the coachman. And they were dismissed, discharged, let go, bounced by the master just before he left for Spain, where he is presently buying up art masterpieces for a song."

Mortimer stared at the glass of port wine the maid set before him. "Ah me. Fortune has frowned upon us, again. We counted our chickens before they were fricasseed. . . . Well, well, well . . . And may I ask, sir, where their grandparents might have gone?"

"An excellent question. So many people seem to want to know that," said Slickens, as he poured more wine for himself.

"Many?" asked Mortimer.

"But I don't have the foggiest idea. They simply disappeared into the blue. Right, Miss Cogglesworth?"

Miss Cogglesworth was munching on some crackers spread with caviar. "Mmm . . . the blue, it was . . ."

"Quite so. Pass me some more of that caviar, Miss Cogglesworth, if you please," said Slickens. "Excellent with port. Must bring up another bottle. *I've* never been to Spain. But the master takes Jenkins along instead of me. I've never been anywhere." Slickens took his glass of port and raised it high. "To Jenkins. May he choke to death on a Spanish olive."

"Hear, hear!" said Miss Cogglesworth, raising her own glass.

"Cogglesworth, how about fetching another half dozen jars of imported caviar from the larder. And give some to our guests. Nothing but the best. Tell me, Mr. Wintergrass, just where are you staying in this great city of ours?"

"The name's Wintergreen. I do believe we'll stop at the Union Square Hotel. Right near all the theaters."

"Excellent establishment," said Slickens. "Do stay there. I'll send you a crate of caviar and a case of port wine. It's a promise. Compliments of my master. The stupid lout! No offense. After he finishes cheating the Spaniards out of their art treasures, he'll move on to Italy. And Jenkins goes with him. Some valet Jenkins is. Doesn't even know how to draw a bath properly. Not too hot. Not too cold. Right down the middle. But does the master take me along on his travels? Does he, Cogglesworth?"

"Never," said Cogglesworth.

"And why not?" asked Slickens.

" 'Cause he's a stupid lout."

"Precisely. Don't speak with your mouth full, Cogglesworth. There are children present. Children who are staying at the Union Square Hotel, right? And who are to be sent ten pounds of the finest imported Swiss chocolates, along with the caviar and wine, compliments of the house. But don't forget, make sure you're at the Union Square Hotel, because that's where all the tidbits are going to be sent."

"Very good," said Mortimer. "The Union Square Hotel it will be, to be sure. But tell me, why were they fired? I mean the Baineses."

"I believe it was the squirrel that finally did it. What do you think, Cogglesworth?"

"Stupid lout," said Cogglesworth, finishing off another glass of port. "To your health!"

"Yes, it was the squirrel. When they left, they took that squirrel with their cats and pigeons, and that was the last we saw of them. In my opinion, it was good riddance. No offense."

"Did you say cats and pigeons?" asked Mortimer.

"Certainly. It took ten years, but the master finally kicked them out. The wine cellar, the maid's room, the attic storage closet, full of pigeons. Baines picked them up all over town. It was a rare day that he didn't return with a sick pigeon or a starving cat up there with him on the coach seat. Or a mongrel dog. But it was the squirrel that finally did it. A squirrel racing across a banquet table is not your best dessert surprise. If Mrs. Baines hadn't been such a good cook, the master would have fired them both years ago. But he was in love with her duck à la Baines and her strawberry shortcake. And so he looked the other way, when the pigeons flew by."

"Ah me," said Mortimer. "The world does not always treat the kindly very kindly."

"How true," agreed Slickens. "Look at me.

Kindest man alive. An expert at drawing baths. And he takes *Jenkins* to Europe. But I'll get to travel abroad; you can count on it."

Mortimer flicked a drop of caviar from his tie. "No doubt, no doubt . . . Ah, ahem . . . One small favor. If a certain lady named Vootch should ever stop by here, you needn't mention that you've seen us."

"Vootch? Oh. Hmm . . . Did you say Vootch?" asked Slickens.

"Vootch it was," replied Mortimer.

"Certainly. I mean certainly *not*. No offense. I would never say a word. After all, why should she know you're staying at the Union Square Hotel. That's private between us. My mouth is sealed."

"I thank you," said Mortimer, as he stood up. "Well, we must be going. Good day to you sir, and thank you again. And if you care to see the greatest magic show in the history of New York, watch your local paper for time and place. . . . And now, my diminutive friends, it's time for a good steak dinner and a night of sleep."

Mortimer whistled a little tune as they walked around the side of the mansion to the wagon. But Joshua couldn't help feeling troubled. There was something wrong about Slickens. Something wrong. Slickens was just too darned slick.

13. THE LUXURIES
OF NEW YORK LIVING

Courage," said Mortimer as they drove off. "We shall search and scour the city of New York City until we find your noble grandelders, or my name isn't Mortimer Q. W. I have two hundred and thirty-four dollars from our balloon sale tucked neatly away in all my pockets. That sum can tide us over quite tidily for some time. In fact, tonight you're going to sleep in a hotel. In a real room. On a real bed. And tomorrow I will seek a booking at one of the better theaters. My act can't miss; the money will pour in. Naturally, you will pay off all your past, present, and future debts by working as my stage assistants. Agreed?"

"You mean I have to go onstage with millions of people watching?" asked Amy.

"Fear not. It's much less frightening than going up in a balloon. Much shorter distance to fall."

"But what about Aunt Vootch?" asked Joshua. "She'll spot us easy."

"Let us cross that barn when we come to it. Now I think we can all use some good steaks, medium rare. Clean your fingernails, my friends. We are about to dine in style."

Mortimer drove up to Thirty-fourth Street and across toward Broadway. At Herald Square, they passed beneath an elevated railroad line. Overhead a small locomotive with three cars roared by, while the iron support pillars trembled.

"Calm, calm," Mortimer called to Chrysanthemum. "That's only the Sixth Avenue El. A mere trifle."

"I can see the bottom of the train!" Amy shouted. "Joshua, look up! Look! There's cinders falling down!"

"Well, well," said Mortimer. "After a week, you won't notice it at all. Just part of the scenery. Like the fire brigade."

Mortimer drove up Broadway and stopped the wagon in front of a restaurant with a sign shaped like a steer. The sign read:

KLUTCHER'S STEAK HOUSE,
ESTABLISHED 1843.

It was dim inside the restaurant and heavy with dark oak paneling and thick red carpets. In one corner, on a raised platform, a violinist was playing a waltz tune. Joshua wondered whether this was the restaurant Mortimer had dreamed about back on the prairie, the restaurant in which the violinist had stolen his hat.

Mortimer asked if there was a table for four. "Ah, certainly sir," said the headwaiter. "And would you care to check your hat?"

"Never. My hat and I are inseparable. That's why I've ordered a table for four. One seat is for my chapeau."

"But sir, we don't permit hats in the dining room—"

"Nonsense, my good man. My hat will be joining us for dinner. It's not a heavy eater, but it's very fussy."

The bewildered headwaiter showed them to their table. Mortimer placed the hat very carefully on the extra chair and ordered three large filet mignons and a small one for the hat, all medium rare. "We shall require plenty of French fries and onion rings. And smother our steaks with mushrooms. I'll have a schooner of your best root beer, chilled please, and my three friends, here, will have large lemonades with quantities of ice and sugar."

As soon as the waiter left with his order, Amy asked, "Can your hat really eat? Because if it can, how come you're not afraid that it'll bite your head off someday while you're wearing it?"

"Nonsense, nonsense. Hats don't eat; anyone knows that. If my hat could eat, it would have kept all the bacon and taffy for itself. We'll split the fourth steak three ways, amongst ourselves."

The waiter returned with a huge tray of dishes and carefully placed the small steak in front of the hat. Then he looked at Mortimer curiously, shook his head several times, and walked away.

The steaks were the best Amy and Joshua

had ever eaten. And with the violin music and elegant silverware, the well-dressed people and red-jacketed waiters, Amy felt as if she had indeed become a millionaire's granddaughter after all.

As she finished the last of her dinner, Amy looked at Mortimer's hat, sitting upturned on its chair. It was missing everything, she thought. What an awful time to be nothing but a hat, even a magic one. She took a bit of steak and dropped it into the hat. Now at least it had had a tiny taste of their dinner.

But Mortimer had seen her. "No, no," he said. "You have a good heart, young lady. And my hat does look a bit starved at times. But when I clap it back on my head, that steak is going to land on top of me."

Mortimer put his hand in the hat. "Now where did that go? Did you really drop a slice of steak in there, or were you doing a little sleight of hand?"

"I don't know any sleight of hand, except how to cheat at checkers," she said.

"So *that's* how you win," Joshua whispered angrily. "I should've known. I'll never play you any checkers again!"

"Ah children, let us not behave like children in public. By George Quincy Washington, I can't find that steak at all, at all." Mortimer cut another piece of steak and tossed it into the hat, then looked inside. "Well, well. It's disappeared, too."

He quickly cut up the small steak and dropped the slices into the hat, one after another, as the waiter came to clear the table. "Not so fast, my good fellow," said Mortimer. "My hat is a slow eater. Some hats are, you know." The waiter shook his head again and walked away. And every so often he looked back toward their table and shook his head some more.

"Friends, it's incredible. Our hat has decided to gain some nourishment. Ah me. One can never tell which way the tree will tumble, when it comes to magic hats. They're very temperamental. I wonder if it would care for some coffee and strudel."

Mortimer ordered milk and chocolate cake for Amy and Joshua, and coffee and strudel for himself and the hat. By now, all the waiters and many of the diners were glancing toward their table.

"I'm afraid we're onstage already, friends. Our unusual dining companion is drawing some attention. Most embarrassing. Still, one must not neglect a starving hat." And Mortimer poured some hot coffee into the hat, very delicately. Then he looked inside.

"Oh great flying flamingoes! My chapeau is soaking wet! There you are! Temperamental! It's decided to skip dessert. Well, well. Finish up quickly, friends. The headwaiter looks like he's ready to call the police!"

Mortimer paid the bill by plunking four silver dollars onto the table. Then he took a bottle of Wintergreen's All-Season Health Tonic and set it next to the silver dollars.

"There we are. I always leave a little tonic as a tip. A healthy waiter means a happy restaurant. Let us depart."

Chrysanthemum was waiting patiently for them outside. She nodded her head happily as they climbed onto the wagon. By now the gas lamps were glowing up and down Broadway, for the long shadows of the buildings had touched one another and blended into evening darkness. Mortimer put his hat on his lap and took the reins. "I hope my hat decides to dry out rapidly," he said. "Till then I shall bare my scalp to the rays of the moon. I do not enjoy wearing a soggy chapeau, even if it is magically inclined. . . . Gee yap, Chrysanthemum! We're off to the Union Square Hotel, where you'll get a warm stable and a royal meal."

As Mortimer drove through the streets, Joshua and Amy counted windows in the same way that they'd counted clouds during their balloon flight. But they soon gave up; there were just too many windows. So they decided to count only "twins," which was the name they gave to double windows set close together. The "twins" looked like pairs of yellow eyes; they reminded Amy of jack-o'-lanterns. At one point she thought she could make out an entire face formed by the lit windows of a tall building. It would have been perfect except that the nose was one window too low.

As they followed Broadway down to Union Square, Mortimer maneuvered Chrysanthemum between clanging horse-drawn trolleys, rattling wagons, graceful carriages, and regal coaches. At Union Square the traffic grew even heavier, for many larger avenues emptied into the huge open arena. In the center of the square was a magnificent statue of Washington astride an enormous bronze horse.

"Ah, here we are," said Mortimer. "Look straight ahead, Chrysanthemum. There's the finest statue of a horse in the northern hemisphere. Grand spectacle. And atop the horse is the uncle of our country, George Quincy Washington himself, in person. You see him there, victorious, after the Battle of Gettysburg. I would take off my hat, but it's already off."

Mortimer drove the wagon once around the square, then stopped in front of the Union Square Hotel. As they entered the hotel, doormen and bellhops leaped into action, opening doors and taking packages.

Chrysanthemum was led to the hotel's private stables for the night, while they were shown to their room. It was a large elegant room on the third floor, with French windows that opened onto a balcony overlooking the square. After Mortimer tested the beds for bounciness, they all went out on the balcony to see the statue and watch the endless flow of wagons and carriages. And every so often they saw a horse-drawn two-level trolley go by. Amy took her drawing book and made some quick sketches of the bustling scene below. Her hand flew; there were so many new things to see and draw.

"Look! Look!" said Joshua, suddenly. "There, on that trolley!"

"What? Where? Who?" Mortimer stared at the traffic below.

"No . . . I guess not," said Joshua. "For a second I thought I saw Aunt Vootch."

"Impossible," said Mortimer. "There's a million people in this city. Even if she were here, she'd be just another noodle in the haystack. . . . And now, friends, it's time for sleep. You can have the big bed and I'll plunk down on the little one by the wall."

They went back into the room and shut the windows for the night. Then Amy and Joshua took turns in the bathroom. But first Mortimer had to show them how to work the toilet, for in all their lives they had never seen a flush toilet. In the rural towns of South Dakota, everyone used outhouses.

"Ah yes," said Mortimer. "The luxuries of New York living overwhelm one's body and soul, do they not? And if I told you that all you have to do is turn that handle there on the sink to get a glass of water, what would you think of that?"

"If Aunt Vootch had her house in New York," said Joshua, "maybe she wouldn't have to work us like she did. We could've just played checkers all day. If Amy wasn't such a cheater, I mean. Everything here is so easy."

"Ah no," said Mortimer. "It never works that way. If you had been living here, she would have made you clean the sink, fetch ice from the ice wagon, and run up and down the stairs to buy this from that store and to exchange that from this store and it would have been even more work, and twice as confusing. Now let's make haste while the moon shines; it's well past your bedtime."

Within ten minutes all the gas lamps in the room had been turned off and everyone was under the covers, ready for sleep. Joshua heard Amy's even breathing and, in another moment, the muffled snoring of Mortimer. They were both asleep. And Mortimer's hat was resting at the foot of his bed. There it was, waiting to be tested one more time. The moonlight through the window shone on the smooth silk top. It seemed as if the hat wanted to be noticed, wanted him to try his luck again.

Joshua clenched his fists, trying to decide. What could go wrong in a hotel room? They weren't floating over Dakota anymore, a mile above the solid earth. And the hat was right there. Right there.

Joshua tiptoed to the bureau and took one of the silver-plated guns. Then he carefully took the hat from the bed, holding it by the edge of the brim. He held the gun in front of the hat and whispered, "Okay, hat. Would you please give me some bullets for my gun? Please? If you please? Pretty please? Thank you."

Then he put the gun down and took a deep, tense breath. Slowly, he let his hand down into the hat. He thought he heard a muffled panting, as if from a dog. Or a wolf. Or—

There was a sudden pincerlike pain in his hand! Something was nipping his hand! He pulled back abruptly and dropped the hat. The panting stopped.

Trembling, Joshua placed the hat back on the bed precisely where it had been. His heart thumped in his chest like an angry fist. He went to the window and examined his hand by moonlight. There was no blood, but there were indentations on the back and palm as if an animal had bitten down, then released him.

The hat *was* ferocious! He would never put his hand in again. Not ever! Maybe the hat liked Amy, but it hated him. Why? Why? Because of the bullets? His wanting those bullets? But he wasn't a bandit. He wasn't going to shoot the hat as that bandit had done. Didn't the hat understand?

Joshua recalled Mortimer's story about the trapeze artist in the circus and the tiger. That man had wanted gold. Wasn't that what Mortimer had told them? Gold and bullets . . . Joshua sighed. He'd been lucky he'd just gotten nipped. *He* could have lost his whole hand, too.

He decided to say nothing to Mortimer or Amy. What was the sense in telling them how dumb he'd been, doing something that stupid again. No, he would say nothing. And he'd stay away from that hat, no matter what.

14. THE MAGIC HAT COMPANY

That next morning Mortimer brushed his jacket and hat, put on a pair of white gloves, then announced that Amy and Joshua were to behave like upper-cruller children for the next hour, while he attended to business. They were not to watch the horse-drawn trolleys from the balcony until they'd put the pillows and blankets back in place on the bed. And they were to put the entire room in good order.

"We must not let this place become a goat garden. Wish me luck, friends. I'm off to Brinkerhoff, the theatrical agent. Maybe he can place my act as the featured attraction in a variety show. Farewell. And remember not to forget to remember to tidy up."

When he was out the door, Amy said to Joshua, "He's getting as bad as Aunt Vootch, almost. Tidy up, clean up, fix up."

"You're loco," said Joshua. "He practically never tells us to do anything. But still—we might as well have some fun first."

Joshua wondered if he should tell Amy about his trouble with the hat last night. But no, it was like a bad dream that he'd rather just forget. "Let's have some fun," he repeated.

He moved the two beds closer together, then leaped from one to the other. Amy joined in, and they spent the next hour jumping, bouncing, bumping, and diving back and forth between beds. Then, when she'd grown tired of jumping, Amy reminded Joshua of the incredible faucets on the sink, with their endless supply of water.

Joshua bet Amy that he could fill the sink faster than it could drain. They opened the faucets all the way, and the sink filled to overflowing. Then they submerged the drinking glasses, upside down, to turn them into diving bells. When the bathroom floor was thoroughly soaked, they returned to the beds.

Joshua moved the beds farther apart to make the jump more difficult. "Here I come!" he called. "The greatest leap in the stellar system. By the world-famous jumper: Joshua Q. Winterbaines."

Joshua sprang through the air in a sensational leap, but just as he landed on the other bed, Mortimer burst into the room. Joshua stretched out and lay there, pretending to be asleep.

"Wake up, young man!" Mortimer shouted. "I've gotten a booking! We're in! The Palace Theater! A most superior establishment. Unfortunately, there are seventeen other acts in the show; I'm on for only six minutes. And there's no available dressing room. Still, I'm going to be on the stage of the Palace Theater! My parents, may they rest in peace, never played the Palace. They would be proud! Mortimer Q. Wintergreen has arrived at last!"

"Yowee!" shouted Amy. "You'll be famous!"

"He's already famous!" added Joshua.

"Only in Dakota," said Mortimer. "In New York, it doesn't hurt to be acquainted with a bit of luck. A sword swallower in the show cut his throat rather badly, and we're the replacement. Yes indeed. We go on tonight. But enough! We have serious business ahead! We're going to start our search for your grandparents this morning. My, my. The room looks neat as a pin now. Nice work."

Mortimer studied a map of Manhattan to find a likely spot to begin their search. He turned the map sideways and upside down, then finally drew a large red circle near the bottom.

"We will begin here!" he said. "On the great broad way called—you guessed it, friends—Broadway."

Within half an hour they were on the wagon going slowly down Broadway. Mortimer stopped in front of an employment agency that had a COOK WANTED sign on display.

"We must be detectives," he said, as they climbed the rickety stairs of the A.A.A. Ace Agency. "We must find clues. Maybe your grandmother obtained another cook's job with the help of an agency."

A man behind the desk in the musty office sniffed as they entered. "Yes, yes? Children looking for jobs, eh? Can you sew buttonholes? Ten cents an hour for buttonholes. Twelve hours a day. Good money. If you want an A.A.A. job, always come to me, Albert Anthony Ambrose Ace. I congratulate you, sir. Your son and daughter are in good hands."

"No, no," said Mortimer. "These children are employed by *me*. They'll be working two hours a night, holding my hat and fetching my magic wand."

Holding it by the edge of the brim, thought Joshua. At a distance.

"What!" said A.A.A. Ace. "Kids working only two hours a night? Waste! Sheer waste. Healthy youngsters like that. A complete waste." And A.A.A. Ace sniffed again.

"See here, Mister Ace, I'm trying to locate a Mrs. Baines," said Mortimer. "She's a cook. Excellent with raspberry shortcake, so I'm told. Have you, perchance, found employment for her recently?"

"Baines? Let me see. I'll have to check my B's. Very nice letter, *B*." He went to a tall filing cabinet and took out a manila folder with a large *B* on it. Then he returned to his desk and started thumbing through the papers in the folder. "Mmm . . . Backer, short-order cook. Bagson, window washer . . . Aha! Baines! How much is the information worth to you?"

"A silver dollar."

Mortimer felt in a pocket, and Mr. Ace leaned forward as he heard the sound of coins jingling.

"Payable in advance," said A.A.A. Ace.

Mortimer put a silver dollar on the desk, and Mr. Ace immediately pocketed it. Then he pulled out a sheet from the folder. "Baines: cook, highest recommendations, will work nights and weekends, accepted job at 328 Fifth Avenue, December fifteenth, 1883. How's that? Ten years ago, and still on my records."

"It's not worth a plugged penny. That's the job she was just fired from! Don't you have anything new?"

"Sorry. That's it. Call again. Your son and daughter look like terrific buttonhole sewers. Bring them around. I can get the shirts for them. And remember, for the snob type of job, it's A.A.A. Ace, the happy employment place."

"Mr. Ace?" Joshua said as they were about to leave.

"Yes, young man? How can I be of service?"

"I dropped my pet rattlesnake into your desk drawer while you went to that cabinet before, to get the B's. Would you mind watching it for me for a few days?"

"Your pet *what*! Where? Which drawer! How am I going to use my desk! I can't get to my references! To my jobs! I'll have you thrown in jail! Police! *POLICE!*"

Mortimer, Amy and Joshua rushed down to the wagon and rode off, while A.A.A. Ace continued to shout from the window above. "Well, well," said Mortimer. "I was about to ask that child-selling scoundrel to dip into my hat for a little treat. But your make-believe snake is better than a real one. Yes indeed. He'll think it's around somewhere, and jump at every sound for weeks."

As they continued down Broadway, Mortimer stopped at one agency after another, but A.A.A. Ace appeared to be the only agent who had ever heard of the Baineses. They had gone as far as Canal Street when Mortimer remembered that he had to rent costumes. "We cannot appear on the stage in our street clothes. We must rent outfits with spangles and sequins and silver trim. But don't worry; we'll continue our search tomorrow."

Mortimer turned uptown, toward the hotel, for he knew of an excellent theatrical-costume shop called Koehler's near Union Square. By now Chrysanthemum had grown quite used to the heavy traffic. She wove in and out among the carriages and trolleys like the fastest firehorse, and they reached Koehler's within twenty minutes.

Amy had a fine time in the costume shop, trying on dresses that seemed to shine with a light of their own. But Joshua hated fussing with clothes, and he picked the first jacket that fit. Mortimer finally decided that they should all dress completely in white, and Joshua had to be fitted all over again.

Before returning to the hotel, Mortimer stopped at a delicatessen and ordered three pastrami sandwiches on rye bread. Amy and Joshua had never heard of this kind of sandwich before. Then Mortimer asked for three kosher pickles, medium sour, and Amy and Joshua were puzzled again. Food in New York was very different from food in South Dakota, where a pickle was a pickle, and that was that.

Back in the hotel room, they quickly changed into their costumes. Their white glittering outfits seemed to transform the room itself into a stage.

While Amy and Joshua ate their sandwiches and made wry faces from the sour pickles, Mortimer explained their part in the act. He showed them how to hold his hat—by the very edge, to Joshua's relief—and where to stand so the hat would always be visible to the audience. He led them through the entire act several times, from start to finish to bow, though he didn't actually take anything out of the hat.

"Must save it for the grand opening," he said. "I am certain my hat's in good spirits today. After all, it isn't every hat that can become a famous star overnight. Very well.

We are ready. It's time to go. Break a leg! That's what we say when we wish somebody in show business good luck. Break a leg! The reason is simple. If I said good luck, you'd probably end up breaking a leg."

Just then there was a knock at the door, and a voice called, "Packages! Packages for Room 308!" Mortimer opened the door, and a bellhop holding a stack of packages that reached to his eyes took a step into the room. "Where shall I put them, sir?" he asked.

"On top of the bed, young man." Mortimer opened a bureau drawer and took out a bottle of his health tonic. He pressed it into the bellhop's hand. "There you are! A little gratuity for your service. When you've finished this, you'll be able to carry three times as much."

There was a note attached to one of the packages. Mortimer opened it and read aloud, " 'To Winter Q. Mortimergreen!' Well, well, confusion everywhere. 'Here's the wine, caviar, and candy I promised to send. Drink a toast to poor old Mr. and Mrs. Baines, for me. Yours truly, Slickens.' Splendid! We'll have a little opening-night party for ourselves after the show. But right now we've got to be on our way. It's an hour to curtain time."

Mortimer took his hat and gave it a little tap. "Break a leg. Or I should say, break a brim." Then he clapped it onto his head and made a quick check of the room to see if he'd forgotten anything. "Ah yes," he said, "my white gloves. Essential for first-rate magic."

As they went down the stairs and crossed the lobby, the hotel guests stared at their dazzling white outfits. "Must be the latest fashion," said an elderly lady to her husband. "Nothing but white. I'm so glad I'm too old to care."

They pushed past the huge glass doors that led to the avenue. The doorman looked at them with raised eyebrows.

"Shall I call a carriage, sir?"

"Never," Mortimer answered. "Have the stableboy fetch my horse and wagon."

"Your wagon!" said the doorman. "Is that old thing for a costume ball, sir? You *are* going to a costume ball, I assume?"

"Absolutely. We're going dressed as snowflakes, and my cow, Chrysanthemum, will be going dressed as a horse. Now have my wagon brought round before I lose my temperament and turn you into an icicle."

"Certainly sir," said the doorman, as he walked haughtily away.

"Ah me," said Mortimer. "I don't think I'll tip him at all. He'll never know what Wintergreen's All-Season Health Tonic could have done for his shoes. Yes, friends, my health tonic can also be used as a shoe polish. Shines them up like the dickens."

Within a few moments the stableboy returned with the horse and wagon. Everyone scrambled on, and Mortimer called, "Gee yap, Chrysanthemum!" Then with a glance toward the doorman, he added loudly, "And please do not *moo*, Chrysanthemum! Remember, we are in costume now."

The Palace Theater was only a few blocks away. Mortimer didn't drive up to the front entrance but, rather, went down a side street to the door used by actors and stagehands. He tied Chrysanthemum to the post of a gas lamp, and gave her a special treat of oats and sliced apples.

Then Mortimer opened the heavy metal door marked STAGE ENTRANCE. Amy had expected to see chandeliers and beautiful carpets, but the rear of the theater was a dim jumble of passageways and dressing rooms. Mortimer followed a corridor that led to the wings, an open area at the side of the stage.

From the wings, everything happening on the stage could be seen, though sideways. The show was about to start, and the performers in the first act, a group of acrobats, were warming up with handsprings and somersaults. Then a bell rang, and they took their places on the stage, forming a human pyramid with three men on the bottom, two on their shoulders, and one at the very top. The top man raised an arm as a signal to the stagehands, and the curtain went up.

Amy could see the audience as they applauded the dramatic opening. There seemed to be no end to the rows of faces; there were two balconies in the rear that went so high that Amy, from the wings, couldn't see to the top. The acrobats had started their act, but all she could think about was that mass of faces out front.

"Fine theater," whispered Mortimer. "One of the largest in the city. If you feel a little weak in the knees at this time, do not worry. It's normal. Even I feel a slight trembling in the little finger of my left hand."

A large man chewing on the butt of a cigar came toward them and asked, "You Wintergreen?"

"The very same. Mortimer Q."

"Okay. You go on after the seal act, see."

"Couldn't I possibly follow a singer or a dance team?"

"The seals. That's your slot. After the seals. Don't worry. The seal act stinks. After them, anything looks great. Okay?"

The acrobats finished their act to a round of applause. Then a large card was placed on an easel facing the audience. On the card, written in gold glitter, were the words:

TIMMY TAP,

THE DANCE MARVEL.

A man who had been humming and doing little dance steps near Joshua skipped out onto the stage and started tap dancing, while the orchestra played some jumpy, bouncy tunes. As he danced, he talked to the audience about his dancing, "Now that's easy. . . . Now that's hard. . . . That's something I'll have to try someday. . . ." The audience loved it.

One act followed another without a moment between: a comedian, a man with trained doves that flew around the theater and then returned to the stage, a man and woman who sang while they danced. Mortimer called them a song-and-dance team. "Ah, my dear parents sang and danced just like that," he said. "If only they could be here now."

Then the ramps and platforms were set up for the seal act. A card that read SELBY'S SUPER SEALS was placed on the easel. Amy and Joshua had never seen live seals before, but they were so nervous they could scarcely watch, for their act was next.

"Calm, calm," said Mortimer. "Look how relaxed those seals are. They are thinking of the fish they'll get after the show, and I suggest you think about that big package of candy in our hotel room."

The seals flip-flopped up the ramps and

balanced balls on their snouts. Then Mr. Selby, their trainer, threw a ball to one of them, and the seal bumped it back. Soon the trainer was playing ball with all five seals, while the audience laughed and applauded.

Then another big card was placed on the easel. It read:

MORTIMER WINTERGREEN
AND HIS MAGIC HAT COMPANY.

Amy and Joshua ran out to the center of the stage and bowed just as Mortimer had shown them, then gestured toward the wings. And out stepped Mortimer Wintergreen, tipping his hat to the audience as he walked to center stage.

"Ah yes," said Mortimer. "Ladies and gentlemen, girls, boys, cats, and dogs . . . My, my, there are no dogs or cats with us tonight. Six hundred and twelve apologies. I am no longer performing in a barn." The audience tittered, but Joshua and Amy felt embarrassed. The audience had laughed in a different way at the seals and the comedian.

"And now my friends," Mortimer contin-ued, "I would like your kindliest attention, if you please. The young man at my left is going to hand me my magic wand. And I, in turn, am going to hand him my hat. You will note that nothing else will pass between us but a hat and a wand. Observe!"

With great ceremony, Mortimer removed his hat. The audience was silent now, leaning forward, watching. Then Mortimer and Joshua exchanged hat and wand. Joshua held the hat at the very edge of the brim.

"Thusly," said Mortimer. "Now I'm going to ask the young lady, here, to help the young man hold the hat. . . . There we are. They're holding it between them, and for good reason. The hat may get rather heavy. One never knows. I've seen large creatures leap from it, in my time. Toads, tigers, and turtles have all emerged from that innocent chapeau."

The audience tittered again, and Joshua felt himself blushing. They didn't believe Mortimer. Well, they'd find out, soon enough. He wished Mortimer would pull out a swarm of angry bees, one bee for each smirking face beyond the footlights. Or maybe that panting animal . . .

"Now ladies and gentlemen, boys and girls, watch me very closely. I pass my magic wand over the hat once, twice, thrice. I repeat the magic words 'Albert Anthony Ambrose Ace' and put my hand down into the hat, like this. And . . . ahem . . . and . . ."

Mortimer whispered to Amy and Joshua. "Nothing there! Jiggle the hat a little." Then he called loudly, "Yes indeed, folks. As you can see, this is a plain, ordinary magic hat which sometimes drops off to sleep, like anyone else. . . . Ahem . . . Yes . . . Well, well . . ."

The tittering and laughter from the audience was changing to catcalls and booing. Mortimer dipped his hand into the hat once more. "Albert Anthony Ambrose Ace!"

"Hey, magician!" someone called from the second balcony. "Let's hear you sing!"

"Hey! Can you do a soft-shoe dance?"

Mortimer bent down and whispered to the hat while the shouts spread from one end of the theater to the other.

"Take him off! Bring on the juggling act! Go back to your barn! Show it to the cows!" Suddenly Amy saw an egg hurtling toward her from the direction of the balcony. It smashed against the stage behind her.

Mortimer kept trying to get the hat to work, but the theater had gone wild. That first egg proved to be the opening shot of a barrage of rotten eggs, spoiled tomatoes, overripe apples, stale buns, and other assorted groceries.

"Everyone's saved their garbage for the Palace Theater," called Mortimer as he ducked and dodged and bowed and desperately shook the hat again and again.

"Ring down the curtain!" the man with the cigar shouted from the wings. "Ring 'er down!"

The huge curtain descended, nearly hitting Joshua on the head as he jumped back to avoid a well-aimed grapefruit. But the curtain had come down too late; Mortimer, Amy, and Joshua were covered with the remains of spoiled tomatoes and rotten eggs.

The man with the cigar screamed at Mortimer, "You phony! Get out of this theater and stay out! And those brats, too! Go back to the country, you bumpkin! This is the big time! No place for amateurs! The money I wasted on that sign! And look at my stage!

Covered with rotten eggs! It'll take half an hour to clean it up. Meantime they'll wreck the theater." He shouted to an assistant, "Hey! Put an act out in front of the curtain. Anything!" Then again to Mortimer, "Out, OUT, OUT! Beat it, before I beat you up!"

Outside, in the alley, Mortimer wiped some of the egg and tomato off Amy and Joshua. "Ah me, ah me. My career as the world's greatest magician has been smashed like a . . . I regret to say, like a rotten egg. Let's retreat to the hotel and get washed up. We'll sneak up the rear fire exit so we won't be seen in this condition."

Mortimer drove slowly back. Not a word was spoken by anyone, but Joshua noticed in the yellow light of the gas lamps that there were tears running down Mortimer's cheeks. And his hat was on the wagon floor, instead of on his head.

15. NO OFFENSE, NO OFFENSE

Mortimer stopped the wagon in front of a small stable behind the Union Square Hotel. An old man on night duty came out, unhitched Chrysanthemum, and led her into the stable. But Mortimer seemed not to notice; he sat on the horseless wagon with head bowed.

"Mr. Mortimer, we're there," said Amy.

"I'm nowhere at all. Nowhere at all. However, one must go on. Courage, Wintergreen, courage . . ."

As they climbed down from the wagon, Joshua saw that Mortimer hadn't bothered to pick up his hat.

"Your hat!" he called.

"Ah me. I won't be needing it tonight.

And it won't be needing me. It can sleep right here on the wagon."

"But . . . it's your magic hat . . ." said Joshua. "Even if it wrecked your show. Anybody could wreck a show." Mortimer seemed not to hear. Joshua continued, "Maybe it had a reason. Remember what you said when I pulled out that rope that tied us to the ground? That maybe it was for the best? What if your hat knows what to do better than we think? Like when it wouldn't give me any bu— I mean—What I'm saying is shouldn't we forgive it and take it with us?"

"Do as you wish," said Mortimer. "But *you'll* have to take care of it. I am not on happy terms with my chapeau. In a word, the friendship is over. If I could find that ship's captain, I'd sell it back to him." Mortimer sighed and turned to go.

Joshua took the hat very gingerly from the wagon and followed Mortimer and Amy down the dark street. He held the hat carefully at the edges. Whether the hat knew what was best or not, he wasn't going to take any chances with it.

Mortimer led them through the hotel's rear

fire exit and up the iron stairway. They managed to reach their room without being seen, and in a few minutes their once-shimmering costumes lay in a tangled heap on the bathroom floor.

"We cannot possibly sleep with that odoriferous wardrobe in our room," said Mortimer. "Dump the whole pile on the balcony, Joshua, and shut the glass doors. Tomorrow I'll have them cleaned and returned. I shall not be needing them any longer. My days as a magician are over. I plan to sell the hat, tomorrow, to the first old-clothes peddler I see."

Joshua wished he could think of something, anything, to say to cheer him up. "Mr. Mortimer . . . I think you're a great magician no matter what happened."

"So do I!" said Amy. "I think you're a great *everything*! If we can't find Grandma and Grandpa, I—we!—would like to stay with you, if you'll let us."

"Ah . . . well, well, well . . . Those are indeed kindly words," said Mortimer. "The mutual feeling, I assure you, is mutual."

"Excuse me a minute," said Amy. "There's

something I want to do!" She took her sketchbook and pencils from the bureau, then sat down abruptly and started sketching.

Joshua watched her with amazement. She had started to sketch Mortimer's face. "Don't move for a minute, Mr. Mortimer," she said.

"Ah me, I do believe I'm being asked to pose for my portrait. I am honored, young lady, to my depths."

"But Amy," Joshua said, "you swore you were never going to draw a person again, and—"

"I changed my mind!" said Amy. "Mr. Mortimer's my friend."

"Well, well," said Mortimer. "I am touched to the core. . . . By Jupiter, I said we'd have a party after the show, and we will! Open Slickens' presents, Joshua! Let's pretend that we're the hit. . . ." Mortimer hesitated, then continued with a break in his voice. "The hit of—the city of New York City. Ah me . . ."

Joshua tore off all the wrappings and plunged into the boxes of candy. He dumped a pile into Amy's lap as she sat sketching. While they sampled the candy, Mortimer ceremoniously opened a bottle of port wine and filled a small goblet. He raised his glass in a toast. "Here's to Amy and Joshua Baines. My good friends. May you never own a magic hat or a magic shoe to make you miserable. May you never own a magic anything. Then you'll live to be as happy as the day is short."

Mortimer drank the wine and nibbled on a piece of candy. But he stared at his wine glass with a tired, lost look. "Ah me . . . Ah me . . . I think I'll get some sleep. This wine has numbed my brain. And my ill fortune has numbed my soul. Eat some of that candy for me. Good night, my small companions." Mortimer lay down, and within half a minute he was snoring loudly.

Amy started a new sketch of Mortimer asleep, while Joshua continued sampling one candy after another. Some had nuts inside, some had sweet syrup, and some were solid chocolate. But it didn't take very long before he felt faintly sick. He stopped midway through chewing a caramel.

"I never figured I'd be sick of eating candy," he said. "But I am."

Just then there was a knock at the door. Joshua looked back at Mortimer, but he was sound asleep. "Guess we'd better answer. Who is it?"

A voice said, "It's me, Slickens, the butler. I forgot to send you the box of imported toy soldiers on horseback with cannons, swords, and rifles. You needn't open the door; I'll just set it down here, outside. Good night."

"Yahoo!" called Joshua. "That's some present. We'd better wake up Mr. Mortimer. Mr. Mortimer! Hey, Mr. Mortimer!" But Mortimer snored on. "Oh well, we can show it to him in the morning."

Joshua opened the door. There was a sudden push, and Slickens, the butler, charged into the room. He looked around wildly. "No offense. No offense. But a man has to earn a living somehow. I'm to be paid rather handsomely for this little job. No offense, but I must take the money where it comes from. Otherwise, how would I ever get to travel to Europe?"

Then a familiar voice called, "You won't even get down the stairs unless you do your job, numbskull!" And there, in the doorway, stood Aunt Vootch, holding her whip. "Grab them!" she shouted.

Amy screamed, but her cry was muffled by Slickens' hand. For in a great sweeping motion, he placed his arms around both Joshua and Amy, one on either side. Amy wriggled and twisted her head and tried to bite him, but it was impossible. Slickens had too firm a grip.

"Nicely planned," said Aunt Vootch. "Putting a sleeping potion in all the wine bottles was a masterstroke. Ah! That hat! There it is! Now we have everything! Let's get these runaways down to the carriage, Slickens. We'll take the rear fire exit."

Aunt Vootch checked the corridor to see whether anyone was outside, then signaled all clear to Slickens. Slickens rushed Amy and Joshua out of the room and down the hall. Joshua twisted and tried to escape, but Slickens squeezed his head harder and harder, till he felt it would burst.

"No offense, no offense," Slickens murmured as he forced them down the iron stairway, his hands still over their mouths. But Amy managed to bite one of his fingers and Slickens called out, "Aarrrrhh!"

Aunt Vootch cracked Slickens on his head with the butt end of her whip. "Shut up, you cabbage! You'll wake up the entire hotel!"

Slickens lurched out to the street, dazed from the blow to his head. He stumbled and his hand slipped from Amy's mouth. Amy screamed, and Slickens instantly covered her mouth again, only to have his finger bitten a second time. He forced back a yell and called "Unnnnngg!" instead.

"Cabbage!" hissed Aunt Vootch. A man walking by on the other side of the street turned to see what was causing all the strange sounds. Aunt Vootch said loudly, so he would overhear, "Naughty children! You'd better let your dear father take you home now! And never, never stay out so late again!" The passerby continued on his way.

Slickens forced the children up into an elegant open carriage and sat between them, hands still over their mouths. Then, after carefully placing Mortimer's hat on her lap, Aunt Vootch cracked her whip over the horses.

As she turned the carriage onto Broadway, she started to sing, "La tee dum la, te la tee dum . . . This has been a fine evening for me. Yes, you delinquents, a fine evening. I have you *and* I have this hat or machine or whatever it is. And we're in time for the late train. The express to Chicago and points west. How nice it was that I got to Slickens before you. You've done well, Slickens, you cabbage, you. Very well. La tee dee dum . . ."

"I just did what you told me to do," said Slickens. "I always do my job well. When someone says, 'Make my bath medium warm,' why, medium warm it is. And when someone says, 'Don't tell them their grandparents live in a hovel on Broome Street,' then I don't tell them. I follow instructions, as any good butler should."

Just then the carriage jolted over a pile of loose cobblestones, and the magic hat fell sideways and rolled off Aunt Vootch's lap.

She was so busy whipping the horses again and again that she didn't notice.

Joshua took a deep breath. Although he was thoroughly frightened—of Slickens, of Aunt Vootch, of the hat—there was no time to think. He had to act now! Right now! He plunged forward, pulling Slickens' hand with him, and grabbed the magic hat. Please hat, he thought, be my friend! Please! We need you! I'm sorry about the bullets. Please!

He thrust his hand down in and felt a piece of cloth.

"Stop him!" Aunt Vootch shouted, hitting Joshua's arm with her whip.

Joshua yanked at the cloth in the hat with all his might. There was a great whooshing noise, and out of the hat, as if shot from a cannon, came yards and yards of cloth, swirling and fluttering and covering them all. More cloth and more spewed forth, followed by great lengths of rope. As they struggled to free themselves, the avalanche of cloth began to unfold above their heads, filling and bellying out like the sails of a ship, or a circus tent, or . . . a balloon. Indeed, it was a balloon, lifting upward as it expanded. And on its side, in huge blue letters, were the words

CALCOTT'S CARNIVAL BALLOONS,
THE BEST IN SOUTH DAKOTA.

"It's a trick!" shouted Aunt Vootch. "I'm tangled in the ropes! They've trapped me! Slickens! Slickens! Help!"

"No offense!" called Slickens. "No offense! But I'm caught in the ropes, too!"

The huge gas bag bobbed down, up, and down again. Then it shot straight up over lower Broadway. And dangling below, held fast by its guy ropes, were Slickens and Aunt Vootch.

"*Yiii!*" screamed Aunt Vootch as she rose above the buildings. "Help, Slickens! Help!" She started whipping the balloon above her.

Slickens seemed to have lost his sense, for he kept shouting, over and over, "Hooray! I'm off to Europe at last! Hooray! I'm off to Europe at last!"

Amy and Joshua watched until the balloon

became a little black moon retreating toward the east and the shouts grew so faint that they seemed like the cooing of doves. Then, without saying a word, Joshua carefully, lovingly, placed the hat on the seat, took the reins, and turned the carriage back toward the hotel.

16. BROOME STREET

my couldn't wait to tell Mortimer about the great balloon rescue and about how brave Joshua had been. And more: The hat Mortimer had planned to sell to a peddler was still as magic as ever. The hat was actually a hero!

"I'll bet Aunt Vootch is over the Atlantic Ocean by now," Joshua said as they went through the lobby. "And all she's got with her up there is her whip."

"*And* Mr. Slickens," added Amy. "Poor Mr. Slickens. What a way to travel to Europe."

"Poor! He almost broke my head!"

As they approached their room, they could hear Mortimer's snoring from the hallway.

"He's got the loudest snores I ever heard," said Amy.

"That's 'cause they gave him knockout drops, or something, in the wine. It makes you sleep twice as fast."

"That's loco. Nobody can sleep twice as fast."

"Not usually. But that's what knockout drops do. And they make you sleep for a day or more. So I don't know how we're gonna be able to wake him."

In the room, Mortimer still lay on top of the bed; he hadn't so much as moved a finger. And his snoring was, indeed, thunderous.

"Maybe we better call a doctor," Amy suggested.

"What good's a doctor? You're supposed to sleep it off. Haven't you ever read any books about pirates or bandits or things? They always sleep it off. And the next day they wake up with their legs chained, down in the hold of a ship, and rats climbing all over them. Now let's get to sleep. We'll surprise him tomorrow morning."

But it was Mortimer who surprised them, for when they awoke in the morning, he was already at the sink, pouring water over his head.

"Oh me, oh my, oh me," he groaned. "I must have had too much wine. Oh my aching noggin."

"Good morning," said Amy brightly, trying hard not to giggle out loud at the fantastic news they were about to tell him.

"Good . . . ohhh . . . morning. Ohhh, my head . . ."

"We have some news for you," Amy sang.

"Just so long as it is not loud. Whisper it. I cannot take loud noises until I've had some very black coffee."

"We saw Aunt Vootch," Joshua said, turning away so Mortimer couldn't see the smile he was trying to force back.

"Worry, worry. You're seeing things in the dark. . . . Oh my poor bean."

"And your hat saw her, too," Amy continued. They couldn't hold back any longer. Amy and Joshua burst out with all that had happened, shouting over one another to be first to tell.

"Too loud! Whisper, please," said Mortimer. "My head feels like a cannonball after it's been fired through the side of a concrete fort. Now, were you saying that Joshua, brave lad, grabbed the hat and pulled out one of our balloons?"

When they'd finished telling the story, Mortimer picked up his hat and kissed it. "Forgive me, my faithful friend. A thousand and seven pardons. You've behaved nobly. It shall be an honor evermore to place you upon my head—if my head ever stops aching."

"And now we know where Grandma and Grandpa live," said Joshua. "It's Broome Street. Slickens let it slip out."

"Splendid!" said Mortimer. "We will give Broome Street a clean sweep as soon as we've had a bit of nourishment."

Mortimer ordered some breakfast to be sent up to their room, including a pot of black coffee. Then he took all the bottles of wine and poured their contents down the sink. "Bad riddance to good rubbish. I should have had nothing but orange juice in the first place. Well, well, well. In a little while we'll be off to Broome Street to find your dear old grandelders. Right after we drop our stage costumes off to be de-smelled. Let us start packing our possessions, such as they are."

Mortimer paid the hotel bill with some of the nickels, dimes, and quarters he had gotten from their wagon sale back in Dakota. The hotel manager glared at the growing pile of coins on the counter.

"Ah, that's a relief. It was weighing down all my pockets. And here, sir, is a little something for you." Mortimer took a bottle of health tonic from his pocket and placed it on top of the coins.

"Thank you very much." The manager took the bottle and tossed it into the trash can behind him. "Good day."

As Mortimer, Amy, and Joshua walked across the lobby to the big glass door, they overheard the bellhops, standing in a line near the entrance. The bellhops evidently wanted to be overheard, for they were speaking quite loudly.

"Lowlifes! He's paid his bill in pennies."

"You should have heard what they did to their room."

"Flooded it with water."

"He finished off ten bottles of wine in two

nights. The maid saw all the empty bottles in the wastebasket."

"Common trash. Good riddance."

Mortimer tipped his hat to the bellhops, then took a gold coin from his jacket pocket and tossed it toward them. The coin rolled along the carpeted floor. "With my compliments. A little tip. You may draw lots for it."

The bellhops leaped for the coin, pushing and punching one another. Mortimer, without a second glance, led Amy and Joshua out to the street.

"I didn't know you had gold pieces," said Amy. "Why waste it on *them?*"

"Ah, you're right. I should have offered a few to you." Mortimer gave Amy a handful of gold coins from his jacket pocket. She immediately saw what they were: chocolate coins covered with gold foil, from Slickens' boxes of candy.

"I trust they've discovered by now what it means to leap before you look," said Mortimer.

He sent Joshua to fetch Chrysanthemum and the wagon while he left the costumes with a laundress who lived just above the stable. And in a few minutes they were all on the wagon heading downtown toward Broome Street.

As they rode past Houston Street, into one of the older sections of New York, the streets grew narrower and more crowded. There were children everywhere. They played in the streets and on the fire escapes; they shouted from windows and rooftops. They seemed to hang from the very sky.

Mortimer had to maneuver past peddlers with their pushcarts, past milk wagons, ice wagons, vegetable carts, umbrella menders' carts and scissor grinders' carts. Indeed, the streets were so mobbed, it would have taken less time had they walked.

The people looked very strange to Amy and Joshua. There were old women dressed in black, and young girls with bright kerchiefs covering their heads. Some of the boys wore little black caps without brims. And everyone looked poorer than the poorest children in South Dakota.

"Look about you," said Mortimer. "It's like taking a trip around the world. These people came here from every country in the universe. Russia, Italy, Poland, Ireland, Greece, even China. Everywhere. In fact, the only really strange people here are you. Who else on the Lower East Side of New York came from South Dakota? But do not fear, my fine-fuddled friends. No one will notice; they'll just think you're from some country they've never heard of. Which, of course, you are."

"They look so poor," said Amy. "And sort of sick and skinny and all. Like that boy over there."

"Ah yes, no doubt. Life isn't easy on the Lower East Side. In South Dakota even poor people have a little piece of land, or a couple of cows, or a horse. Here, all they have is each other."

"That's something," said Joshua.

"True enough . . . Oh pickles! I've been struck!" Mortimer looked up at a tenement building across the street. "Did you see who did it?"

"Did what?" Joshua asked.

"Something bounced upon my bean. Did those children up there throw a ball down at us from that fire escape?"

"I didn't see anything," said Joshua. "Did it hit your hat?"

"My hat? I completely forgot. I'm wearing my hat, again. Something must have hit me from within. My hat has bombarded me while resting on my noggin. It does that from time to time, as you may know."

Mortimer took his hat off, and there, on top of his head, was a hard, doughnut-shaped roll. He examined it carefully. "This, friends, is called a bagel. Delicious with cream cheese. Would you care to taste it?"

Amy was about to take a bite when she saw a girl looking at her. The girl's dress was ragged and her arms were as thin as the spindles on a straight-back chair. As the wagon passed by, Amy reached over and handed the bagel to her.

"Thank you! Thank you!" the girl called to Amy. "Look! They're giving out bagels!" she shouted to her friends.

A group of children ran toward the slowly moving wagon. "Me! Please, me!" they called, with their hands outstretched.

"Well, well," said Mortimer. "Let's see if there's another bagel in my bonnet for this crowd of tiny tots." Mortimer stopped the wagon, then reached into his hat and took out an orange.

"Me! Please! Please!" begged the children. Mortimer tossed the orange to a sad-looking boy, alone behind the others. The boy caught it and smiled.

"He does it with tricks!" a girl shouted. "He's a magician!"

"My chapeau is definitely being friendly again," Mortimer said to Amy and Joshua. "Most definitely. Therefore, let us proceed!"

Mortimer reached into the hat again and again. As apples, balls, cookies, jump ropes, tops, and whistles appeared one after another, he tossed them to the children crowding the wagon like hungry birds. But after several minutes, the hat started giving bottle caps, orange skins, and bits of broken cups. Mortimer stopped and clapped the hat back on his head. He announced to the children, "Fear not! I shall be back soon, my friends! But my hat needs a rest. It is not used to being in such a good mood! Do not worry! We shall be back! I thank you kindly."

As Mortimer called "Gee yap" to Chrysanthemum, he felt something hard drop on his head, again. He reached under his hat and retrieved the object.

"It's a pocketknife," said Amy.

"Look! It's *my* pocketknife!" Joshua shouted. "The one I lost in the mud that night, in Aunt Vootch's pigpen. Remember, Amy?"

"By Alexander Q. Hamilton! My hat's getting to like you like the dickens! Here's your knife, young man. But now, get ready. That's Broome Street, right there ahead of us. Prepare to keep your eyes, ears and noses open for any sign of your grandparents. Meantime, I'll ask someone on the street if they know where their domicile might be."

Mortimer turned the wagon onto Broome Street and pulled over to the curb. He called to an old man pushing a heavy cart full of fish. "Ah, my dear fish man, I would like to ask you a small question."

The man stopped pushing his cart. "How did you know my name? Hah? How?" he asked.

"I don't know your name," Mortimer answered.

"You do! Fishman! That's me. J. C. Fishman, selling the finest fresh flounder in New York. How many pounds do you want? Four? Six? Two growing children. They have to eat fish to see in the dark. Fish will make you strong. Tall. Smart. Eat!"

Amy whispered into Mortimer's ear, "He sounds sort of like you, Mr. Mortimer, when you sell your health tonic."

"Indeed, indeed. And can your flounder cure hiccups, pray tell?"

"No," said Mr. Fishman. "Not unless you choke on a bone first."

"Well, well. I have a little bottle of tonic here that can cure hiccups in the wink of a pinkie. Fifty cents the bottle. Two for seventy-five."

"Aha," said Fishman. "But, *but*, can your tonic cure common liver complaint? Try a pound of my sturgeon. Your liver will be like new."

"Very nice. But can your fish cure bald-ness? Answer *that* if you please, sir."

"I'll answer that when you tell me if your tonic can cure color blindness."

"I'll answer that when you tell me if your

fish can cure snakebites?" said Mortimer, his face turning redder and redder.

"Snakebites? Why should eating fish cure snakebites? You may as well ask if eating snakes can cure fishbites. The thing to do is simple. Don't bite the snake in the first place. Here, have a free flounder. Your children need it. They look pale."

"Thank you most kindly," said Mortimer. "Unfortunately, we have nowhere to cook it. But have a couple of bottles of tonic. It makes an excellent sauce for fried filet of cod. Gives it that extra tang." Mortimer handed him several bottles. "Now then, Mr. Fishman, I'd like to ask whether you've seen or heard of a Mr. and Mrs. Baines? I am told that they live somewhere along Broome Street. They are elderly."

"Baines . . . Baines . . . Do they eat fish?"

"I couldn't truly say, sir. But the lady probably cooks fish. She is, by profession, a cook."

"Ah. A cook. I love to cook. Come to my humble apartment and I'll cook you a fish dinner like you've never seen."

"My regrets to your kind offer. But we're

searching for these children's grandpater and grandmater and we must push on. The name is Baines."

Mr. Fishman thought some more as he stared down at his fish. "Baines . . . Yes . . . No . . . Let me think. . . . Maybe . . . Is that Baines with a B like in *banana,* or Paines with a P like in *piano?*"

"With a B like bursting bubbles broke on the baby's bib."

"Never heard of them," said Mr. Fishman. "But when you find them, if they're color-blind, tell them they need fish. And tell them that, with Fishman, the fish is always as fresh as a firecracker."

"Indeed, I will. Good day, sir. And many thanks."

17. AN ORANGE MOON

As they rode slowly along Broome Street, Amy and Joshua kept careful watch while Mortimer called up toward the windows, "Baines! We are searching for Baines! Baines!"

His voice blended with other cries in the street. A vegetable man was calling out, "Here! Potat-ooes! Cauliflowerrr! Caaarrots! Here!" And an old-clothes man called up, "Buy! Sell! Hats! Coats! Suits! Dresses! Old! New! Buy! Sell!"

The street echoed with "Baines! We are searching for—" "Caaarrots!" "Old—" "Caaarrots!" "Baines!" "Hats! Coats!" "Pota-tooes!" "Baines!"

Mortimer kept calling, block after block,

until he was quite hoarse. "Ah me," he said. "No one seems to answer to Baines, whether it's Baines as in *banana* or Paines as in *piano*. I am beaten, friends. I regret to admit it, but it may be time to go to the police. They know everything about everyone, every-where."

"You don't need the police," said Joshua, as he studied a tenement building. "It's what you said yesterday: We have to be detectives. And you've got one. Me."

"Is that so, my whippersnapperish young friend? Well, a detective needs a clue or two or three. Put that in your smoke and pipe it."

"Okay. Look at that window up there." Joshua pointed toward the building he was watching. "See anything kind of strange?"

"No . . . It's a plain, ordinary open win-dow."

"Keep watching."

Amy and Mortimer looked at the window, but nothing seemed unusual. Then a pigeon flew out from the window and rose up and perched on the edge of the rooftop, among a dozen other pigeons. And within a few seconds, one of the other pigeons flew down to the window and in.

"By Joshua Quincy Baines! I've heard of people keeping trained pigeons on their roofs, but not in their kitchens. You may have hit the jackrabbit! Let's find out."

Mortimer and the children crossed the street and entered the tenement. It was an old, decrepit building with a stairway that sagged and walls that tilted slightly to the left. The dim hallway had a musty smell of damp pipes and worn carpets. As they climbed to the third floor, the stairway trembled under their feet and the handrail wobbled back and forth.

On the third-floor landing, Mortimer knocked at the nearest door. After a moment, a man wearing a work apron peeked out at them.

"Yes? Hurry up! Hurry up!" said the man. "I'm busy. Busy, busy, busy. I have a hundred buttons to make in the next hour. I'm on my grays and greens today. I've no time to spare. No time. None. What do you want? Hurry. Good day." And he slammed the door in their faces.

Mortimer knocked again and the button maker reappeared. "Well? Well, well, well? What?"

"We're looking for Mr. and Mrs. Baines," said Mortimer. "Do they live in one of the apartments on this floor, pray tell?"

"Baines! Did you say Baines! His pigeons have been eating my buttons. My yellows and whites. They think they're corn kernels. Blast! Good day!"

"Aha," said Mortimer. "We'll try next door."

Mortimer knocked and a large woman wearing a red robe appeared. "Ah yes. We're looking for a Mr. and Mrs. Baines—"

"You from the madhouse?" the woman asked. "They're over there." She pointed to a door across the hallway. "Sitting with their pigeons on the floor. Take them away. And good riddance. Can't hang my wash out on the roof with all those pigeons. Disgrace. What's this city coming to? Madhouse. Take them away."

"We'll have a look," said Mortimer.

"Look? No need. They're cracked. Pity. But

life must go on. Are you going to use force?"

"We shall see what we shall see," said Mortimer.

"Good. If you use force, ring my bell. Would enjoy, truly. Like to see a good show, time to time. Here's luck." And she closed the door and latched it with a click.

"Prepare, children, for the worst. With all their problems, your dear old grandelders may, indeed, have tangled their telegraph wires. We'll soon know."

Mortimer rapped on the door, and as he did so, it swung open. The room within was filled with cooing pigeons, fluttering and landing and flying out the window. And seated on the floor, in the center of the room, were an old man and woman. A clean white tablecloth was spread out before them.

Mortimer tipped his hat. "Ah, good day to you good people. A thousand pardons, but the door swung open. . . . I see you're feeding the pigeons."

The old man looked up at Mortimer. "Feeding them? We're not feeding them. *They're* feeding *us.*"

"I beg your pardon?"

"We're having lunch," said the woman. "Would you care to join us? Our little friends can always find a few more crusts and crumbs."

"They've been feeding us for weeks," added the man. "Ever since they saw how we were starving here. We used to help them. Now they're helping us. I count my friends by the hundreds. What other man can say that in this day and age?"

"May I present three more friends. My name is Wintergreen. Mortimer Q. And these children are none other than Amy and Joshua Baines. Your very own kith and kin."

"You're fooling us," said Mrs. Baines. "They're in South Dakota living with their kind, lovable Aunty Vootch."

"Tell them, children," said Mortimer. "Start from the beginning, while I round up a small feast for your unfortunate grandparents."

In no time at all, Mr. and Mrs. Baines could see that Joshua and Amy really were Joshua and Amy. They immediately cried, laughed, and cried again, and kissed the children a dozen times each.

The pigeons fluttered about the children,

perching on their heads and shoulders. Amy couldn't help laughing, because their feet tickled, and because she knew she was home.

Mortimer returned, his arms loaded with covered dishes from a nearby restaurant. He spread everything out on the white table-cloth, and everyone had a huge serving of roast beef with baked potatoes. When the pigeons saw that their friends the Baineses had more than enough to eat, they left, one by one. But a few remained in the room, fluttering about and perching on the chan-delier above, like guardian angels.

"I cannot begin to find words enough to thank you, sir," said Mr. Baines. "That was the first solid meal we've had in weeks."

"Tush, tush, and a boot full of slush. It's a pleasure and a privilege, I assure you. As soon as you find work, you can treat *me* to a roast beef dinner."

"Work? We're too old. No one will hire us anymore," said Mr. Baines. "We're ready for the poorhouse!"

"If only we'd saved our money," continued Mrs. Baines, "instead of spending it all on cat food and dog food and sparrow food and squirrel food and I don't know what. We always dreamed of opening a little restaurant, a place where people could feel welcome, even if they brought their pets with them. We'd have a special room where we could feed their dogs and cats in royal style. But . . . we never managed to save a penny."

"Ah, tush and again tush. You're making mountains out of maple syrup. These children and I have managed to earn a penny or two on our eastward voyage. Permit me to present you with the first payment on a restaurant." Mortimer started to unload coins from all his pockets. Quarters, half dollars, and silver dollars piled up on the tablecloth.

"We can't!" said Mrs. Baines.

"We won't!" her husband insisted.

"Nonsense, nonsense. It's merely a loan. You can pay me back when you've made your fortune."

"But we couldn't possibly take your—"

Mortimer didn't let him finish. "See here, sir! I haven't crossed the country with these midget persons merely to see them starve in the great city of New York City. No, no.

Although they are, no doubt, rude, unmannered whippersnappers, always disagreeing with their elders merely to be disagreeable, they are, after all, human at times, though rarely. And they deserve to have a spot of spinach and a plate of pickles from time to time."

At that point, Amy laughed, for she knew Mortimer meant just the opposite. "See that! Laughing at their elders. Terrible! She'll come to a bad end, teaching children in school how to spell *Massachusetts* and *rhinoceros*. A bad end. And now, I must be on my way. Farewell, friends. I must go."

"Could we say good-bye to Chrysanthemum?" asked Amy.

"Certainly. And your sketchbook is still in the wagon. As are those silver-plated six-shooters. Weighing us down unnecessarily."

They all went down the three flights of shaky stairs to the wagon in the street. Amy kissed Chrysanthemum's neck and Joshua smoothed the horse's mane. Mortimer climbed into the wagon and handed the sketchbook to Amy, then gave the guns to Joshua.

Amy immediately tore out the sketches of Mortimer and gave them to him. "These are for you," she said.

"Ah, splendid. A thousand thank you's. Perhaps, someday, you can draw some pictures of yourself and Joshua. For me . . ."

Then Joshua handed his guns back to Mortimer. "I . . . I don't need these anymore. These are for you. You could sell them and use the money, maybe for a steak at that restaurant. For you and the hat . . ."

"Well, well, well. No more guns, eh?" said Mortimer. "It must be my tonic, young man. You seem to have just grown taller. But it is time to depart. Farewell, my friends! Be civil to your grandfolks and do not eat with your feet."

"Good-bye, Mr. Mortimer! Good-bye, Chrysanthemum! Good-bye, hat!" Amy called.

"Thank you for getting us to New York, Mr. Mortimer," Joshua said. "Thank you! And thank you, hat!"

"Nothing at all," said Mortimer. "A mere trifle. To which my hat agrees. Farewell, friends. Farewell. Perhaps I'll see you again when the moon turns orange."

Amy, Joshua, and their grandparents watched as the wagon jolted and bounced down the street.

"Good-bye!" Amy shouted with all her might. "Good-bye!"

Mortimer raised his hat to them without looking back. And there, perched on the top of his head, was a breakfast roll. He took the roll and tossed it to a little girl. As the wagon rattled down the long street, they saw Mortimer dip his hand into his hat, again and again. A crowd of children followed at the side of the wagon, while he tossed out apples and cookies and shiny red tops.

They watched till the wagon blended with all the other carts and wagons in the distance, until Mortimer Wintergreen became a blur among the children and peddlers, the scissor grinders and ice men and vegetable men. Then they turned and went back up the shaky stairs, sad and happy, happy and sad, both at once.

And their new life began. Amy didn't have

the hundred beautiful dresses she'd dreamed of, nor dolls made of china and silk, but she did have a small bedroom all her own from which she could hear her grandparents talking and laughing at night, before she fell asleep. And that, she decided, was all she'd really wanted in the first place.

It was all Joshua wanted, too, but he wouldn't admit it to Amy. If only his grandmother would hug him less, it would be perfect. For now there were friends—friends who listened to his stories of the West and bandits and Indians, and never made fun of his size— and there was New York to feel and see and breathe, and his grandmother's wonderful cooking, and his grandfather's incredible stories of his early years at sea. His stories reminded Amy and Joshua of Mortimer. If only Mortimer would return, everything would be double perfect.

As the months passed, Amy and Joshua helped their grandparents start a restaurant, which they called the Chrysanthemum Inn. And indeed, there was a special room for feeding everyone's cats and dogs, just as their grandparents had wanted. But where was Mortimer?

One morning they discovered a mysterious bag of bagels left at the door of the restaurant, and once they found a box full of flour for flapjacks. And several times there were penknives and colored crayons. But though they watched and waited for an orange moon, or even a hazy yellow moon, Amy and Joshua never saw Mortimer Wintergreen again.

About the Author

MYRON LEVOY was born and raised in New York City, where many of his stories take place. In addition to novels, plays, short stories, and poems for adults, Mr. Levoy is the author of *The Witch of Fourth Street and Other Stories*, a 1972 Book Week Honor Book; the picture book *Penny Tunes and Princesses*, which was illustrated by Ezra Jack Keats; and *Three Friends*. His first novel for young people, the highly acclaimed *Alan and Naomi*, was nominated for a 1980 American Book Award, and has received a number of international awards in Europe. His second novel, *A Shadow Like a Leopard*, was selected as a 1981 ALA Best Book for Young Adults. His most recent novel, *Pictures of Adam*, was a 1986 ALA Best Book for Young Adults.

X